Axing at the Antique Store

NIGHTMARE ARIZONA
PARANORMAL COZY MYSTERIES

BETH DOLGNER

Axing at the Antique Store
Nightmare, Arizona Paranormal Cozy Mysteries, Book Seven
© 2024 Beth Dolgner

Print ISBN-13: 978-1-958587-20-1

Published by Redglare Press
Cover by Dark Mojo Designs
Print Formatting by The Madd Formatter

https://bethdolgner.com

CHAPTER ONE

I was exactly halfway to work when I felt the first raindrop against my cheek. I looked up at the dark clouds just as a gust of wind ruffled my hair. "Please wait," I said to the sky.

In answer, three more fat raindrops hit my face in quick succession.

I should have known better. When I had walked out of my apartment, I had spotted the dark clouds rolling in from the east, and I half turned to go back inside so I could retrieve my car keys. But I had been sitting at my laptop most of the afternoon, and I wanted to move my body a bit.

Plus, it hardly ever rained in the desert. I would be fine, I had told myself.

By the time I arrived at Nightmare Sanctuary Haunted House, it was nearly dark, even though the sun had just slipped behind the mountains on the horizon. The storm had rolled in quickly, and flashes of lightning illuminated the sky over the weathered stone building while the rain pelted me.

If I hadn't been soaking wet, I would have stopped to appreciate the spooky ambience of the former hospital building in the middle of a storm.

I paused at the front doors, the portico sheltering me

from the rain. A particularly loud clap of thunder sounded as I shook myself like a wet dog, trying to fling off as much water as possible. I even leaned over and gave my shoulder-length auburn hair a squeeze.

With a resigned sigh, I pulled open one of the doors and slipped into the Sanctuary's entryway. The room had a tall ceiling, and the sweeping staircase on the left side led up to the second floor, where many of my friends lived.

Justine Abbott was just coming down the stairs, and she stopped short. "Oh, Olivia, you poor thing."

I grimaced. "Do I look that bad?"

"You look scarier than anything we have inside the haunt." Even though she was joking, there was also a sympathetic tone to Justine's voice. She waved a clipboard she had in one hand. "I had you down to work the front door tonight, but I'm going to put you in the lagoon vignette, instead. You can't work in those clothes."

I unzipped my light jacket and pressed a hand against the black Nightmare Sanctuary T-shirt I was wearing underneath. It wasn't as wet as the rest of my outfit, but Justine was right. I needed a complete change of wardrobe.

A shiver worked its way up my spine. I needed to get warm, too. It had been a chilly day, and the cold and wet were going to settle into my bones if I didn't do something about it.

Justine was clearly thinking the same thing, because she was on the move again, issuing orders. "First, you're going to go to the costume room and dry off, then change into your pirate costume. After that, I want you to head to the kitchen and microwave one of the containers of soup."

"Yes, ma'am," I said with a smile.

"Come on. I'll walk with you. You can throw those clothes in the dryer, so they'll be ready to go by the time we close tonight. Didn't anyone tell you we get a lot of rain in January?"

I fell into step next to Justine as we headed down the hallway that led to the costume room, dining room, and other staff-only areas of the Sanctuary. "No one remembered to give me a 'how to survive in the desert' handbook when I arrived in Nightmare."

Soon, I was in the pirate costume I wore on the nights I was assigned to the lagoon vignette. My long red skirt and matching coat felt blissfully warm and dry, and the black blouse underneath, complete with lacy cuffs, added another welcome layer. There was a hairdryer near the makeup station, so by the time I was finished getting into costume, I was completely dry.

I was still cold, though, so I followed Justine's advice and made a beeline for the kitchen, which was off the dining room. By then, it was nearly time for that night's family meeting, and the benches at the long rows of tables were already filling up.

Two minutes later, I was sitting down at one of the benches, too, with a steaming Styrofoam cup of ramen in my hand.

"Not the typical pirate fare," Theo commented casually in greeting. He flashed me a wide smile.

"Not for a pirate vampire like you, maybe," I replied. "I got soaked on the walk here tonight."

Theo nodded knowingly. "The thunder woke me up early. I was going to go out for dinner after work tonight, so I hope the storm blows over."

Going out for dinner, in Theo's case, meant mesmerizing a tourist so he could drink their blood. Since his fangs had been filed down by a vampire hunter, he had to use a small knife, but Theo was careful, so his unwitting donors were never in that much danger.

Justine seemed to have been waiting for me to return

3

from the kitchen, because she stepped up to the podium at the far end of the room right then. "It's raining pretty good right now," she began, throwing me a wry look, "which means it will probably be a slow night for us. So, make the most of the guests we do have, and scare them so much that they feel justified for coming out in this weather."

As Justine went on to make a few announcements and to dole out that night's assignments, I heard the telltale *tick-tick-tick* of claws against the floor behind me. I turned just in time to see Felipe rise up on his hind legs, his gray leathery snout pointed hopefully toward my face. His muddy front paws were just inches from my coat, and I gently pushed him back down onto all fours.

"Sorry, Felipe," I whispered while I stroked his head. "You're in even worse shape than I was."

I heard an annoyed *tsk* and looked up to see Mori, Felipe's owner, frowning at the chupacabra. "Every time it rains," she muttered.

Undeterred, Felipe trotted toward her. Mori gathered her golden silk gown and leaned away from him. Her fangs flashed as she pointed a finger at Felipe. "Stay."

Felipe snorted, turned around, and walked away. I snickered at his defiance, and Mori rolled her intense burnt-orange eyes.

Justine wrapped up soon after, and everyone rose to get ready for the evening. Since I was already dressed, there wasn't much I needed to do, so I chatted with Mori for a bit, then slowly made my way to the lagoon vignette.

Seraphina had beaten me there, and she was swimming somersaults in the glass-fronted water tank that sat next to the prop pirate ship. I walked up to the glass and gave her a wave as her silver siren's tail flashed in the overhead lights. She blew me a kiss right as the lights blinked three times, then went out entirely. The Sanctuary was open for business.

Unfortunately, Justine's prediction that the crowds would be low was accurate. Never had I been so bored at the Sanctuary. Guests came through sporadically, with empty stretches in between that lasted as long as seven minutes. I only knew that because I began timing the gaps between guests on my watch.

The sluggish night was a big contrast to the steady stream of people we'd had coming through during the holidays. From just before Christmas until right after New Year's, we had been slammed every night. The time had flown past, thanks to tourists visiting Nightmare during their holiday break and people in town to see family.

So far, January's business had been steady. It was still tourist season because southern Arizona weather was mild at that time of year. But, as it turned out, a rainy Wednesday night was not good for business.

Theo and I often played a game with each other, taking bets as to how many people we could make scream, or which one of us could make someone sprint wildly out of the vignette first. Seraphina sometimes joined in, which made it even more fun. Even our game, though, couldn't keep me from yawning and glancing at my watch every few minutes.

When I got my break partway through the night, I retreated to the dining room. There was no need to grab my usual snack, since I was still full from the soup, but I did gratefully sit down on a bench. I folded my arms on the table and rested my chin on them.

"You can't be worn out by the flood of guests," Mori said as she gracefully sat down across from me. She brought a cup to her lips, and I instinctively averted my eyes. I still wasn't used to watching the vampires drink blood.

"I had no idea this job could be so boring," I intoned.

"It happens from time to time. Cheer up. Maybe the weather will clear, and tourists will venture out of their hotel rooms."

Mori's optimism was all for nothing, though. Once I had finished my break, the night continued to drag. When we finally closed at midnight, I changed back into my own clothes and prepared to make my way home.

Except, when I opened one of the front doors, I could see raindrops illuminated by the light inside the portico.

I closed the door, turned to my left, and headed down the hallway to Damien Shackleford's office. *I should have stopped by to say hello to him, anyway,* I realized as I approached the door. He and I had been spending so much time together lately that I felt like I had just seen him, but in fact, it had been a full day since we had spoken.

The door was shut, so I knocked lightly, and I instantly heard Damien's muffled voice say, "Come in."

When I walked in, I saw Damien sitting at his expansive oak desk. He had an elbow propped on it, and his face was resting in his hand. He seemed to be staring intently at a stack of papers.

"Everything okay?" I asked tentatively.

Damien looked up, then sighed and sat back in his chair. He gestured toward the papers. "Just doing research into the supernatural black market."

I nodded knowingly. We had reason to believe Damien's father, Baxter, had been abducted because he was a phoenix, and anything phoenix-related—feathers, ashes, and tears included—could fetch a big price on the supernatural community's underground trading scene.

It was the closest to a lead anyone had gotten since Baxter's disappearance nearly a year before, but we still weren't making a lot of headway.

"Do you want to practice?" Damien asked.

"Actually, I was going to ask for a ride home. It's still raining out."

"Of course."

The question about us practicing hung in the air between us. We had been trying to learn more about Damien's supernatural abilities, but we hadn't made any progress in the past month. We were trying to explore his power without the need for him to get upset first—heightened emotions always sparked his abilities—but it was slow-going. In fact, the most we had accomplished lately was Damien sliding a coffee cup across his dining room table.

Damien stood and reached for the gray suit jacket hanging from a coat tree behind his desk.

"You'll need more than that," I warned him.

"I have an umbrella we can share," he assured me. "Let's go."

I turned to walk out just as Fiona rushed in. She was still wearing her costume, a long white gown that made her look every bit the banshee that she was. The diaphanous material seemed to float in her wake as her wide eyes darted between Damien and me.

"Someone is going to die!"

CHAPTER TWO

I gasped, even as I heard Damien behind me ask, "Who?"

Fiona shook her head, her long black hair sliding over her shoulders. "I don't know. Since coming to Nightmare, my flashes are usually about someone with a connection to the Sanctuary."

"Like my neighbor at the motel," I commented. Leonard Evers had been staying downstairs from my apartment at Cowboy's Corral Motor Lodge, and I had been annoyed by his late-night shouting on the phone shortly before he turned up dead.

"Exactly." Fiona moved past me and sank down into one of the oxblood leather chairs in front of Damien's desk. I sat down in the other one as Damien returned to his seat. As a banshee, Fiona could sense when someone was about to die. In her old life in Ireland, she would then appear to that person, so they knew it was time to say their goodbyes.

"I don't get flashes of death as much as I used to," Fiona continued. She sounded sad, and I wondered if she really missed being a harbinger of death. "The longer I'm away from my homeland and the magic there, the more my connection to it fades. Plus, I no longer know who is going to die. It's frustrating, knowing death is coming for someone but being unable to warn them."

Fiona's flashes were for inevitable death. They happened to her once a chain of events had begun that couldn't be stopped, like a fatal illness, or a premeditated murder.

The shiver I felt this time was different than the one I'd had earlier in the evening, which had been from the rain and cold.

"Then we warn everyone," I suggested. "We can tell everyone here and ask them to check up on their loved ones. I know we won't be able to stop the death, but we can at least give some advance notice of it."

Fiona nodded. "That's a good idea, Olivia. I'll go upstairs and knock on everyone's doors. Why don't you two take downstairs?"

"Theo was planning to go out for dinner," I said as I rose.

"I'll call him," Damien said. "You head to the dining room, and I'll catch up."

I agreed and followed Fiona out the door, staying far enough back that I wouldn't step on the hem of her billowing dress. She swept up the staircase as I turned and headed for the dining room.

There was a small group sitting at one of the tables in the dining room, and as I got closer, I could see they all had playing cards in their hands.

"It's not poker night," I said as I walked up.

Zach, our resident werewolf, grinned up at me. "Go Fish."

Despite the gravity of my task, I couldn't help but laugh. A werewolf, a vampire, a wendigo, and two witches were playing a child's card game. I quickly sobered, though. "Fiona had a flash. Since she doesn't know who it's about, we're warning everyone."

Malcolm was sitting closest to me, and he turned to

peer up at me, his eyes dark beads in his skeletal face. "You're worried it might be one of us who will die?"

"Or someone connected to the Sanctuary," I clarified. "You might want to check up on your loved ones."

Mori put down her cards and swept one arm around the table. "All of my loved ones are here in this building."

"Same," Malcolm said. "And it's hard to kill a wendigo, so I doubt I'm the one in danger."

Zach mumbled something too low for me to hear, except for one name: Laura. None of us were quite sure if she and Zach were just friends, or if they were dating, but either way, Zach cared a lot about the newest werewolf in Nightmare. "I'll give her a call," he said as he rose and pulled his cell phone out of the back pocket of his jeans. He wandered toward a far corner of the room as he brought the phone up to his ear.

The two witches, Morgan and Madge, looked at each other, and I got the distinct impression they were having a discussion even though neither of them was speaking. Eventually, Morgan shook her head, her wispy white hair bobbing around her wrinkled face. "We will go upstairs and check on Maida."

"But it's doubtful the premonition is about one of us," Madge finished. Nevertheless, there was the slightest look of worry on her beautiful face. She tossed her blond curls over her shoulder and raised her chin. "Still, it's best to be sure."

Soon, it was just Mori and Malcolm who were left at the table.

"Do you want us to help you spread the word?" Malcolm asked. He was already reaching for his black top hat, which was sitting on the bench next to him.

"Fiona is taking the upstairs, and Damien is calling Theo," I said. "I think we're covered."

"But what about you, Olivia?" Mori asked ominously.

I felt a jolt at the question. It hadn't even occurred to me that I could be the one who might die. "Oh, I, um…" I stopped and cleared my throat. "I'm in good health," I finished lamely.

Mori's full red lips turned up, and she laughed softly. "I meant, have you checked on your loved ones?"

I quickly made a mental list. *Mama, Benny, Lucy and her parents…* "Oh, I should call my brother, too," I said to myself. "In the morning," I said louder. "I'll check with Mama and my brother first thing. I don't want to bother anyone in the middle of the night."

Mori and Malcolm stared at me expectantly. "What?" I finally asked.

The two of them exchanged a glance, and Malcolm raised a bony shoulder in a shrug. "We were just wondering if you'll be checking up on Mark."

"Oh. Yeah. I suppose I should call him, too." Mark and I were on better terms now than we had been at the time of our divorce, but I realized the significance of forgetting to put him on my list of loved ones.

I heard the sound of the door, and I turned to see Damien walking in. Thankfully, he hadn't heard what we had just been discussing. He was not a fan of Mark.

"Theo just texted," Damien announced. "He said he was right in the middle of dinner when I called."

Ew.

"I'll talk to Mama first thing in the morning," I told him.

Damien nodded. "I was planning to call her tomorrow, but I suppose it's easiest for you to go up to the office to talk to her in person."

Mama and Benny Dalton ran Cowboy's Corral Motor Lodge, and ever since Mama had confessed to being Damien's aunt, he had really been making an effort to get to know her and Benny. It was sweet.

There was no more we could do, so Damien nodded in the direction of the door. "Come on. The sooner you get to bed, the sooner you'll be up and talking to Mama."

I wished Mori and Malcolm a good night, then followed Damien. In less than ten minutes, I was home. Ten minutes after that, I was in bed. Sleep wasn't moving as efficiently as I was, unfortunately, and it was a long time before I stopped worrying enough to drift off.

My alarm was set for eight o'clock, which was ridiculously early for me. When I had been living in Nashville and working for a marketing firm, I was up at six thirty every morning. At the Sanctuary, though, my "office hours" were seven in the evening until midnight, so I typically got up around ten each morning.

I flicked the switch on my coffeemaker with only one bleary eye open, then quickly dressed. I didn't want to waste any time getting to the motel office, and I was so anxious to ensure Mama and her family were safe that I was even willing to forego coffee for the moment. It would be waiting for me when I came back.

Cowboy's Corral had two wings that ran back from the road and a connecting wing at the back of the property. A parking lot filled the space between the U-shape. Up front, near the road, was the two-story cinder block building that was the motel's office.

The bell above the glass door tinkled merrily as I hurried in.

"Good morning!" Mama called out right before her head appeared above the Formica countertop. She had been sitting at her desk behind it.

"I hope so," I answered.

Mama tilted her head and looked at me curiously. "Your hair is a mess. What happened?"

I lifted a hand self-consciously. "Oh, I forgot to brush it, that's all."

Mama pursed her lips, and she narrowed her bright-blue eyes.

Mama was incredibly perceptive. Well, psychic, really, but she had resisted her abilities when they first began to manifest, so she came off as unbelievably intuitive more than psychic. The look she was giving me clearly said she knew I had more to tell her.

"And Fiona had a flash last night. Someone is going to die, but she doesn't know who. I came to make sure you and your family are okay."

"Well, Benny didn't choke on his bacon and eggs this morning," Mama said thoughtfully. "I'll call Nick right now."

I waited while Mama called her son, and I could hear the false cheeriness in her voice as she said she was just checking in. "Call it a mother's instinct," she hedged. Nick didn't know about the supernatural world, and Mama obviously didn't want to say someone's death was imminent because a banshee had said so.

Mama hung up a few minutes later and sighed. "Nick says he's good. Mia headed to the hair salon early to get prepped for her first appointment, and she dropped Lucy at school on the way."

I let out my own sigh. "Thanks. I'm sorry to worry you with this."

Mama waved a hand dismissively. "It's not my first rodeo. Between Fiona and the witches, I've been on more than one deathwatch."

Mama's face suddenly clouded over. "I wonder…"

"You wonder what?" I asked, feeling my heart give a nervous lurch.

"I hope it's not about Baxter." Mama bit her lip worriedly. We already knew Damien's father was in trouble, and since Baxter was her brother-in-law, Mama wanted him to be found safe and sound as much as anyone else.

My phone rang before I could respond, and my first, wild thought was that Damien was calling to tell me something about Baxter. I pulled the phone out of my pocket and saw that it was, in fact, Damien calling me.

I answered with, "What happened to him?"

"Who?"

"Your dad."

"You know as much as I do." Damien sounded confused, and he added, "Did I wake you up?"

"No, I'm at the motel office with Mama. Sorry. She just said she hopes Fiona's flash wasn't about Baxter, so when you called…"

"You thought I might have gotten bad news about him," Damien finished for me. "No. However, what I'm calling you about does have to do with him. Gunnar's friend with ties to the supernatural black market just called him and said he would be here sometime late this morning. You want to head to the Sanctuary around lunchtime to meet him?"

I quickly agreed, and once I filled Mama in, she said exactly what I was thinking. "This is good. If Baxter really was taken by a black-market dealer, then we might be one step closer to finding him."

After that, I had plenty of time for coffee and to call my brother. I even called to check on Mark. Both of them said my sudden concern for their mortality was unsettling, but they assured me they were doing fine.

I got to the Sanctuary at noon on the dot. I found Damien, Gunnar, Malcolm, and a man I had never seen before in the dining room. The man had pale skin, and his black hair was slicked back flat against his scalp. When he turned and smiled at me, I saw he had about twice as many teeth showing as the average person would. They were long and narrow, and I thought of a shark's teeth.

Gunnar flexed his sinewy wings and gestured at the man with a muscular arm. "Olivia, this is Orin."

Mama got what she called vibes from people, and I wondered what she would make of Orin. He felt sinister.

"So you're the conjuror," Orin said, stepping toward me and extending a hand. His grip was strong, and his fingers felt icy against my skin. "You could get rich on the underground trading scene. You want to travel with me for a bit once I wrap up here?" Orin's glittering brown eyes were intense as he stepped back to give me a once-over. He hungrily looked at me, and I shifted uncomfortably.

Damien deftly stepped between us. "Olivia isn't going anywhere."

Orin closed the distance to Damien until their faces were nearly touching. I could practically feel the sudden tension, and the door behind me rattled ominously as Damien's psychic power began to stir.

"Says who?" Orin asked in a low voice. "You?"

CHAPTER THREE

I had seen Damien upset enough times to know what would happen if he and Orin continued to stare each other down. I put my hand on Damien's bicep and gently pushed him out of the way. At first, he tried to resist, but he soon gave in, even though he never broke eye contact with Orin.

Damien is calm, I repeated to myself several times.

"Damien is right," I said. "I don't have any interest in leaving my job at the Sanctuary."

Orin was the one who finally broke off the staring match, turning to bore his eyes into mine, instead. "No need for anyone to get upset. I'm only telling the truth. You could make a killing selling your services."

Damien was close enough beside me that I felt him stiffen. I reached out to take his hand and found it curled into a fist. Slowly, his fingers relaxed, and I slipped my hand into his.

Orin's eyes flicked downward, and I knew he had noticed. I didn't bother to explain to him that my touch coupled with me conjuring Damien to calm down was the only thing keeping Orin from getting punched with a blast of psychic power. Most of us were badly behaved when we lost our temper. Damien, on the other hand, was down-right dangerous.

He was also, I realized, more protective of me these days. Even though I still suspected he had been jealous of Mark during my ex-husband's brief stay in Nightmare, Damien had never said anything to indicate he had any kind of romantic feelings for me. His actions, though, suggested there might be more to our relationship than simply two people trying to figure out their supernatural abilities together.

Gunnar made a noise that was something like a growl. "Olivia is new to our world, Orin," he said in his gravelly voice. "She prefers to follow the rules, and I don't think she cares to do the kind of conjuring you're picturing."

"A pity," Orin said.

How does Gunnar know what sort of conjuring Orin is thinking of? I had to wonder if Gunnar had ever worked the black market, too. He was a good guy—well, gargoyle—but that didn't mean his past didn't hold a few dirty secrets. Even as I thought that, Gunnar ran his fingers down his broad chest, which resembled gray stone covered with a thin layer of green moss. His head dipped, and I got the feeling he knew exactly what was running through my mind.

"Let's sit down," Malcolm suggested. He had remained calm and quiet since we had come in, though I knew he was ready to spring into action if it was necessary.

We dutifully sat down around the nearest table. Gunnar, Malcolm, and Orin took one side while Damien and I took the other. I had dropped Damien's hand, but as soon as we were settled in, he reached over underneath the table and entwined his fingers with mine.

He's never held my hand that way before.

I was so distracted I barely registered Orin was speaking, and I forced myself to focus.

"Like I told Gunnar, I haven't seen any phoenix wares on the market," Orin said. "Still, there are some strange things going on. One of the factions is looking to make a move. The rumors are still vague, but it sounds like they have some kind of power that will help them get a bigger share of the market."

"Factions?" I asked.

Orin nodded. "The Dire Market has plenty of independent dealers, but much of the commerce is driven by four factions."

I snorted out a laugh. "What, are they the supernatural mafia?"

"That's an apt description," Orin said without a trace of humor. Beside him, Gunnar nodded slowly.

Oh. Okay, then. The supernatural creatures at the Sanctuary were good people, and it was easy for me to forget that, just like regular humans, not everyone in the supernatural world was kind and compassionate. I suppressed a shudder as I wondered just how dark the dark side of the supernatural community might be. I decided I really didn't want to know.

"The Night Runners are the ones at the center of the rumors," Orin continued. "I came here to retrace Baxter's steps. Maybe a local will recognize a description of a Night Runners member, and we can confirm they're the faction behind the abduction." Orin looked at Damien. "Of course, I'll need half of my compensation up front."

"You're charging us to help find Baxter?" I asked, incredulous.

"Of course," Orin said smoothly. "Baxter is a commodity. A client—that would be all of you here at Nightmare Sanctuary—has asked me to track down that commodity. This is a trading deal, like all the others I do."

I opened my mouth to protest that Baxter was a person, not a commodity, but the gentle squeeze of Damien's fingers kept me quiet.

Instead, Damien answered in a voice as measured as Orin's. "Let's go discuss numbers in my office."

"See?" Orin said to me. "Damien recognizes my value. No one else here has the contacts or the knowledge I do. None of you knows what the members of this faction look like. Besides, you don't want me to starve, do you?"

I glanced at the ring on one of Orin's fingers. It was gold and had a line of diamonds marching all the way around the band. He was not in any danger of starving.

When Orin stood, I also noticed the very expensive-looking knife strapped to his right thigh.

Orin saw me looking, and he patted the hilt proudly. "It's a pretty piece, isn't it? That's a mother-of-pearl hilt with carved details, and this knife is worth way more than what I paid. Talk about a steal!"

"Did you find it on the... Dire Market, I think you called it?" I asked.

"Nope. I found it right here in Nightmare. I stopped at an antique store I passed on my way into town. The lady had no idea of this knife's real value. It's got enough silver in it to kill a werewolf!"

I immediately thought of Zach, and I hoped very much that Fiona's flash hadn't been about him. Orin had given me the creeps the second I saw him, but was he as dangerous as I thought he was? After all, he had come to Nightmare to help us find Baxter. Killing someone wouldn't exactly be in his best interests if he wanted to keep us as—in his terms—a client.

No, I told myself firmly. *He's scary-looking, but he's not here to cause trouble.* Orin's comment had just been a way to describe the silver content of the knife, and he had used a measure he knew all of us would understand.

Damien and Orin left, heading for Damien's office, and as soon as the door to the dining room had closed behind them, Gunnar sighed. "I'm sorry," he said. "I should have warned you all that he's rough around the edges."

Malcolm made a small noise that was somewhere

between a sardonic laugh and a judgmental snort. "We're all rough around the edges, in our own way. It would have been nice to have had some forewarning of his arrival, though."

Gunnar nodded. "I sent him a message telling him we were looking for any evidence of phoenix items showing up on the market in the past ten months. I was expecting a reply, not for him to simply show up. I didn't know he was coming until he called me this morning."

"Just how well do you know Orin?" I asked.

"He's more of an acquaintance than a friend."

Gunnar looked as shocked as I was by our strange meeting with Orin, and I wasn't about to accuse him of bringing a potentially dangerous person to the Sanctuary. Orin was trying to help us find Baxter, and, if we were very lucky, he would wind up being a valuable resource for us, even if I didn't like the guy.

"What is he?" I asked. "Surely people who aren't supernatural notice all those teeth he has."

"When he speaks, you barely see his teeth," Malcolm pointed out. "He's clearly learned to hide what he is quite well, and if you got a good look at his teeth, then it was because he wanted you to."

"He wanted to intimidate me," I said. Orin had succeeded in that.

"Or show off," Gunnar suggested. "Orin is a tooth fairy, not to be confused with the type of fairy Clara is or the cute little sprite you thought collected your teeth as a kid. Tooth fairies are fierce, and you don't want to be on the bad side of one. They aren't all that common, and Orin is very proud of that. It makes him feel special."

I had never heard of a real tooth fairy, and I hoped it truly was a rare creature, because I would be happy to never meet another one.

There was a banging noise near the door, and I looked

to see Seraphina, her arms rigid and her fingers curled tightly around the sides of her mobile water tank. Seraphina's skin had a faint green tinge to it, but at the moment, her cheeks were dark and reddish. She looked livid.

Fiona was pushing the tank, and I braced myself. Had the death Fiona had foreseen happened? Was she coming to tell us about it? At least, this time, Fiona was in regular clothes instead of her costume, so she looked less spooky. Unfortunately, she did look angry and upset.

I stood up and extracted myself from the bench. "What's wrong?" I asked, taking a few steps toward them.

Seraphina ignored me, and I realized her eyes were fixed somewhere behind me. As Fiona rolled the tank right past me, I turned to watch.

"What were you thinking?" Seraphina yelled, stabbing a finger in Gunnar's direction. "He's too dangerous to be here!"

Gunnar raised his hands, like he was trying to ward off Seraphina's verbal attack. "I asked him for information about the black market. I didn't know he was going to show up. Orin isn't someone to cross, certainly, but we're all on the same side here."

"No, we're not," Seraphina said, her voice low and icy. "That's the man Fiona rescued me from."

CHAPTER FOUR

No one spoke for what felt like a full minute. We all just stared, open-mouthed, at Seraphina. She was still glaring at Gunnar, but I noticed Fiona had her eyes closed, like she was trying to restrain her own feelings.

It was Malcolm who finally broke the silence, his voice smooth and calm. "I'm sorry to hear that, Sera. Obviously, none of us knew Orin was your captor. We knew you came to the Sanctuary to escape a bad situation, but you never told us his name."

Fiona opened her eyes then, and I was surprised when she looked right at me. Her voice was usually low and husky, but it would rise in pitch when she was upset, reaching full banshee wail if she didn't calm down. I was relieved to hear her tone was only slightly higher than usual. "Olivia doesn't know the story."

Seraphina's shoulders slumped, and she finally relaxed her arms, sinking down a little in her tank. There wasn't much room in it, and she shifted until her back was against one side, her silver tail curled in front of her so her fin lifted out of the water.

"I'm originally from an island in the Caribbean," Seraphina explained to me. "I was kidnapped by a former pirate who traded on the supernatural black market."

I tentatively raised a hand, as if I were in school. "A pirate?"

Seraphina gave me a pointed look. "Yeah. It took me a long time to become friends with Theo. You can understand why I have an inherent distrust of pirates."

"Actually, I was going to ask just how old you are. I guess I never stopped to consider how sirens age."

"Oh, I'm only thirty-two," Seraphina clarified. "Like I said, this guy was a *former* pirate, as in a couple hundred years ago. He's an incubus, so he'll outlive most of us. Even though piracy hadn't been a thing in the Caribbean for two centuries, he still dressed and acted the part." Seraphina scrunched up her pretty features in disgust. "Like, move on, right? Anyway, he lost me to Orin about two months later in a poker game."

"Couldn't you have used your siren"—I waggled my fingers—"skills to free yourself from the pirate? Or from Orin, for that matter?"

"Not when there were charms hanging all around my tank that suppressed my supernatural powers. Some witch made them."

Gunnar must have seen the look of mingled horror and confusion on my face, because he said gently, "Not all witches are good, like our trio here, Olivia. Dark magic abounds on the black market."

"Anyway," Seraphina continued, "both the pirate and Orin would sell my hair for money. Siren hair is really valuable because it's used in a lot of love spells." Despite the horrific story she was telling, she still reached up and patted her golden locks appreciatively.

Fiona took up the story from there. "The pirate lost the poker game against Orin at a bar in Savannah, Georgia, and I was living there at the time. I started hearing rumors about a siren being kept captive, and I couldn't just stand by and do nothing. I went in search of her."

Seraphina craned her neck so she could look up at Fiona, her expression softening. "Fi found me, and we fled."

"I had expected Sera would want to return to the Caribbean, but instead, she asked me to take her to the desert. I thought she was joking until she told me she had heard of a place called Nightmare Sanctuary, where any supernatural creature could find safety."

I gestured toward Seraphina's tank. "But how did you get all the way across the country when you have to be in water?"

"Oh, that was easy," Fiona said with a smile. "I got my hands on a cargo van and rolled the water tank right into the back of it. The hard part was getting here without being followed. We were worried about being tracked every step of the way."

"Fi was going to head back to Georgia once she had delivered me to the Sanctuary," Seraphina said. "By the time we got here, though, she had decided to stick with me."

Fiona leaned down and planted a kiss on the top of Seraphina's head. "I do miss fresh peaches, though."

"Does Orin know you're here, Seraphina?" I asked. My brain was already making plans to hide her or get her out of town as long as Orin was around.

Seraphina shrugged. "I expect he does. Word travels fast in the supernatural community."

Gunnar stood up and began to slowly unfurl his wings. "I'm so sorry," he said once he had pulled them in again, tight against his back. "I didn't know Orin was the one who had done that to you, and I didn't know he was going to come here. I thought all our communication would be done through email."

I really wanted to ask Gunnar how he managed to type

on a keyboard when he had such massive hands and such long, sharp claws.

"As long as he doesn't try to take me back with him when he goes," Seraphina said flatly.

"You don't really think he would do that, do you?" I asked. *Of course he would,* a little voice in my head answered. *You knew he was dangerous as soon as you saw him.*

Malcolm's lips turned up in a sinister smile. "He wouldn't get away with it." His tone was chilling, almost like he wanted Orin to try. *Go ahead, I dare you,* Malcolm seemed to be saying.

It was a dare Orin would lose. He might be dangerous, but Malcolm was probably even more so. The difference between them was that Malcolm was one of the good guys, and I trusted him.

"I'll head to Damien's office right now and tell Orin we're not going to work with him," Gunnar said. He turned to move in the direction of the door, but Seraphina raised a hand to stop him.

"No," she said firmly. "I panicked when I found out he was here, but I know all of you will keep me safe. I want Baxter home, and if Orin can help us do that, then we need to see this through. I'm going to lay low as long as he's around, though."

"We'll assign a security detail to you," Malcolm said. "I'm not the only one here who can take him down if he acts up."

"Okay." Seraphina blew out a breath and looked at Gunnar. "Sorry I hollered at you."

"I would have done the same in your situation."

"We're going to lay low, like Sera said, starting right now." Fiona sighed. "Maybe we'll binge-watch something on TV."

"And I'll stand guard outside your door," Malcolm promised. He rose to follow them.

"How do you get up to your apartment, anyway?" I had never thought to ask before.

"We take the elevator," Seraphina said nonchalantly.

"This place has an elevator?"

Everyone laughed at my obvious surprise, which helped to further bring down the tension in the room. We would all have to keep a close eye on Orin, but he was definitely not going to come between us.

Fiona had rolled Seraphina's tank halfway to the door when I called, "No reports of a death yet?"

Fiona slowed and looked back at me, her face worried. "No. Not yet."

CHAPTER FIVE

Once Fiona, Seraphina, and Malcolm were gone, Gunnar and I had the dining room to ourselves.

"I didn't know," he repeated, more to himself than to me.

I moved around the table and wrapped my arms around Gunnar. He was so tall that I wound up with my cheek pressed against his chest. "She knows it wasn't intentional," I reassured him. "And she knows you're doing everything in your power to find Baxter."

I felt Gunnar's body relax, and he gave me a tight squeeze. "Thanks, Olivia. And here we thought it was bad when your ex-husband showed up in Nightmare."

"Oh, that was much more scary," I said, stepping back and giving Gunnar a wink. "I'll fill Damien in as soon as he and Orin are done. Why don't you go fly off some of your nervous energy? It will be good for you."

"No, I'm going to take up watch with Malcolm. We'll come up with a schedule so someone will always be guarding Seraphina."

Gunnar left, and I plopped down onto the nearest bench. My watch said it was only half past noon. A lot had happened in the past thirty minutes.

The dining room always felt warm and inviting when it was full of my friends, but being in there by myself made the space feel too big. Even with the sunshine streaming through the tall windows along one wall, I felt a chill creeping up my arms.

So, instead of sitting in the dining room, I decided to haunt the hallway to Damien's office, instead. I had just started my fourth lap of the hallway, waiting for the door to his office to finally open, when I heard Zach's voice behind me.

"Do you know how loudly your steps are echoing? Stop pacing and fill me in."

I whirled around and saw Zach's head sticking out of the doorway to his office. His rust-red hair was hanging over his shoulders.

"That tooth fairy showed up here," Zach continued, "and I don't know what's going on, but everything feels really tense."

"You have no idea," I began. I walked closer to Zach and caught him up on everything, from Orin's black-market ties to Seraphina's history with him.

When I was done, Zach gave a low whistle. "I'll go up right now and get in on this security detail for Sera," he said. "You know what you have to do, right?"

I shook my head. Did Zach think I was going to act as a supernatural security guard, too?

"You have to keep Damien from blowing up."

"Oh, that. Yeah, I know. I've been on Damien duty since one minute after I got here today."

"And be careful," Zach added. Even though I knew he was gentle under his grumpy exterior, it was rare for him to sound so concerned. "This guy Orin is bad news, and I don't want you to wind up with a target on your back."

"I'm going to avoid him as much as possible," I promised.

Zach's head bobbed once. "Smart move. Keep me posted on how Damien is dealing with all this." Zach gave me a wave and headed toward the entryway. I tried to picture him, Malcolm, and Gunnar all huddled outside the door to Fiona and Seraphina's apartment upstairs. It was going to be a long day for all of us.

Since Zach had said my footsteps were echoing, and I didn't want Damien hearing me traipsing back and forth down the hall, I moved to the entryway and made laps around it, instead. I even walked back and forth through the brass stanchions and red velvet ropes, like I was in line to head inside the entrance to the haunt.

It was after one o'clock before I saw Orin emerge from the hallway. He barely glanced at me as he went out the front door, and as soon as he was gone, I hustled to Damien's office.

Damien looked a bit ruffled but not upset. His green eyes weren't glowing, which was a positive sign, but his wavy light-brown hair was slightly askew, like he had been running his fingers through it.

"This is going to cost the Sanctuary a lot of money," he said tightly in greeting.

When Damien had first arrived at the Sanctuary to run things in his father's absence, he had expressed concern about the haunt's finances. Whatever Orin's price was, I knew it was only going to add to Damien's stress about the Sanctuary's bank account.

I shut the door behind me, and Damien looked at me closely. "You have bad news."

"How can you tell?" I asked as I sat down in one of the chairs.

"You closed the door, and you have a look on your face, like you're dreading something."

I shut my eyes while I took a long, deep breath, then dove into Seraphina's news. Damien muttered something under his breath when I finished, and he leaned back in his chair and stared at the ceiling. "We all need to watch ourselves around this guy."

"Agreed. Seraphina is going to have a constant security detail. Malcolm, Gunnar, and Zach are working on a schedule right now."

"Good." Damien ran a hand through his hair and leaned forward. "Since I can tell my emotions are on the verge of careening out of control, would you like to practice? It probably won't take much to get me to psychically rearrange every piece of furniture in here."

"I'm not sure I'm calm enough to conjure your control," I admitted. "Orin gives me the creeps, so my own emotions are a little out of whack at the moment. You might break the furniture rather than rearrange it if I'm trying to help you. Besides, I need to get to the grocery store, because I've got a nearly empty fridge. To quote Orin, you don't want me to starve, do you?"

Damien seemed disappointed, but I had been honest with him. I felt so unsettled about the events of the previous hour that I wasn't sure I could focus enough to conjure anything, let alone help Damien direct his power. I told him I might be up for something after work that night and headed out.

I only made it to the entryway before I heard Justine calling my name. I turned to see her hurrying down the stairs. "The guys just filled me in," she said. "It's going to be weird as long as that tooth fairy is here, isn't it?"

"Yes, it is," I heard a high, childlike voice answer.

I looked up to see Clara coming down the stairs at a slower pace. She had a thoughtful look in her violet eyes.

"We're heading to the antique store," Justine told me. "I'm looking for a prop for the revamped hospital scene, and frankly, it will be nice to get away from the drama for a bit. Want to join us?"

"Sure, maybe I can get a pretty knife like the one Orin found there."

Justine and Clara both stared at me blankly, and I told them about the knife he'd said he found at the antique store. When I added the part about it having enough silver to kill a werewolf, Clara let out a little squeak.

"That means it can kill me, too," she said. "If there's any iron in it, then it's doubly dangerous for fairies. I'll let my family know to be careful." Clara's parents owned a bar for supernaturals, which was in the basement below the coffee shop on High Noon Boulevard. I wondered if Orin would even make it through the door if he tried to go there. Silver was as deadly for fairies as it was for werewolves. I assumed tooth fairies were immune to silver, or Orin wouldn't have bought the knife in the first place.

I followed Justine and Clara in my own car, so I could browse antiques before heading on to the grocery store. I hadn't eaten lunch yet, and if I wanted to, then I had to buy the food to begin with.

Mining Town Antiques was on the same road as Cowboy's Corral Motor Lodge, but several miles stood between them. The road was the main highway through Nightmare, and the antique store was on the north end of town, making it one of the first businesses visitors would see as they drove into Nightmare from the direction of the interstate.

The sprawling building looked old and slightly neglected. There were chunks of beige plaster that had fallen off the facade, leaving the brick underneath exposed. Out front, a wooden sign with the name of the store on it was so faded that only the outline of the letters was left.

There were only two other cars in the parking lot when I pulled in behind Justine's car. After I parked, I got out and saw a woman standing at the front door, her forehead pressed against the glass and her hands held up to shade her eyes.

"Are they closed?" Clara asked as we walked up.

The woman straightened up and turned to us with a sour expression. "I've been standing here for twenty minutes. If that woman is taking a bathroom break, then it's the longest one ever. Maybe you'll have better luck." With a huff, the woman turned and moved in the direction of one of the cars.

Even though we had no reason to doubt the door was locked, Justine reached out and pulled on the handle, anyway. When the door didn't give, she mimicked the woman, shading her eyes and peering through the glass.

"The lights are on," Justine noted.

"And the sign says they're open," Clara said, pointing at the sign hanging from a suction cup above Justine's head.

"I don't want to go back to the Sanctuary just yet." Justine sighed. "There's a car here, so someone has to be inside. Maybe it really is the longest bathroom break ever, and whoever is working today will come unlock the door soon."

There were windows on either side of the door, and I peered through a break in the sun-faded yellow gingham curtains covering the window on the right. I didn't want to stand around for a long time, but I also didn't want to miss out on rummaging through antiques with my friends.

I could spot an old sewing machine and a couple of brass lamps in the sliver of a view that I had. My eyes traveled down, and I gasped. I jerked back from the window. "Whoever is in there needs help! I can see a hand on the floor."

Clara moved me aside so she could look, too. "Maybe she fainted. Should we break the window to get in? Or do we call an ambulance?"

"We move the curtains to see what's going on," Justine answered. A moment later, the curtains slid apart as Justine directed her telekinetic ability toward them. It was convenient to have a friend who could move things with her mind so easily.

All three of us let out noises of shock at the scene in front of us. The hand belonged to an old woman, who was sprawled on the floor. It was immediately obvious she was dead.

CHAPTER SIX

Clara made a gagging noise and clapped a hand over her mouth.

Justine grabbed my arm and buried her face in my shoulder. "I'm going to be sick," she mumbled against my blouse.

I just stared, too shocked to look away. It was like I was frozen. "Fiona," I finally said.

"You think her flash was about this woman?" Clara asked weakly. "But what's her connection to the Sanctuary?"

"Well, we're here," Justine said. She lifted her head from my shoulder but kept her face pointed away from the window.

"You think this was our fault?" Clara sounded like she was close to hysterics.

I finally pulled my eyes away from the window and wrapped an arm around Clara's shoulders. "This death was inevitable if Fiona got a flash about it," I said, my voice shaking. "It isn't our fault, but the fault of the horrible, horrible person who did this to her."

An image of Orin's knife rose in my mind. He had said he bought it there just that morning. Had he paid for it, or had he killed for it?

Or, I wondered, had he killed *with* it? Judging by the

state of the woman's body, it was a real possibility. And Orin was connected to the Sanctuary, so that would explain why Fiona might have gotten a premonition of the death.

Death. I shook my head. This wasn't just a death. It was murder.

"Who's calm enough to call the police?" I asked.

"You do it," Clara said.

I pulled my cell phone out of my pocket and dialed. Running into dead bodies was becoming so routine I hardly needed to think for my fingers to punch the correct numbers. No wonder Officer Reyes half suspected I was a secret serial killer.

We didn't have to wait long between the time I made the call and when a police cruiser whipped into the parking lot, the tires squealing. Justine, Clara, and I had all moved away from the window by then, and we took a collective jump backward at the car's fast approach.

And, just my luck, it was Reyes who climbed out of the driver's side once the car came to a halt in front of us.

"Olivia," he said. Only he could make my name sound like a swear word.

"Luis," I answered tightly.

Clara pointed toward the window. "We spotted her on the floor, but the front door is locked."

Reyes peered through the window as the officer who had been in the passenger seat finally caught up to him. The two of them had a brief, quiet conversation before Reyes turned to us.

"I've questioned all of you before, a couple of times," he said perfunctorily. "You know how this process works. Who would like to start?"

"I will," Clara squeaked.

There really wasn't much we could tell Reyes, and we certainly couldn't admit that the woman who had been at the antique store before us hadn't noticed the body, only because Justine had opened the curtains with her mind once the woman had left.

Instead, we told him the rest: we had wanted to go antique shopping, but the door was locked, even though the lights were on and the sign said the store was open. I had looked through the window and noticed a hand.

Since it was such a straightforward story, Reyes was done with us in just a couple of minutes. By then, a second police car and an ambulance had pulled into the parking lot.

The officer who had arrived with Reyes had tried the front door, just like we had, and then he had moved out of my range of vision while I had focused my attention on Reyes and the pen that was flying across his notebook. Now, though, I heard footsteps behind us and looked back to see the second officer coming around the corner of the building.

"The back door is unlocked," he said grimly, a roll of yellow crime scene tape dangling from one hand. "I got it cordoned off, but I haven't been inside yet, since there's no rush."

"All right. Let's get in there and take a look." Reyes let out a loud breath, looking between me and the front window. "You are never in the right place at the right time, are you? You ladies can go. I'll call with any follow-up questions."

I was surprised when Justine piped up. "I've been coming to this place for years, looking for props for the Sanctuary. I'm fairly certain the woman on the floor in there is the owner, Mrs. Knowles, and someone killed her. I'm not going anywhere until I know more."

Reyes gave Justine a warning look, and she added a timid, "Please?"

"Fine," Reyes grumbled. "Whatever we're about to

learn will be town gossip by dinnertime, anyway. You three may as well get a head start. But stay right here and wait for me to come talk to you."

We all quickly agreed, and as soon as Reyes had disappeared around the building, I turned to Justine with wide eyes. "Thanks. But I'm so sorry. I didn't know the owner was a friend of yours."

"Oh, she wasn't," Justine said quickly. "Mrs. Knowles always treated me like, well, like I work at the Sanctuary." There were only a handful of Nightmare residents who knew supernatural creatures really existed, and there were even fewer who knew most of the local ones lived and worked at the Sanctuary. Most of Nightmare's population thought of people who worked at the Sanctuary as odd, at best.

None of us wanted to watch the police do their work, so we moved down to a far end of the parking lot, where a half-dead palm tree gave us a bit of shade. It wasn't hot out, but Clara said something about not wanting to get a sunburn on the tips of her pointed fairy ears. Making small talk seemed disrespectful, somehow, so we mostly stood around and stared at each other.

Finally, after about forty minutes, I spotted Reyes heading in our direction. "Ms. Abbott, how well did you know Cynthia Knowles?" he asked as soon as he reached us, already pulling his small notebook out of his pocket.

"Not well," Justine admitted. "I just knew her from shopping here."

"Do you know if she had any enemies?"

Justine shook her head. "No, sorry. It *is* Mrs. Knowles on the floor, then."

"Yes, and from the looks of it, she was murdered not long before you three arrived. Maybe this morning, or right around lunchtime."

This morning. Those words rang in my head like a

warning bell. Orin had picked up the knife on his way to the Sanctuary, and he had arrived there just before lunchtime.

Of course, I couldn't suggest to Reyes that a tooth fairy had bought a knife off Mrs. Knowles, then possibly murdered her with it. Even if I skipped the tooth fairy part, the information about Orin would bring unwanted attention to the Sanctuary, and I couldn't think of a single reason he would have wanted to kill a complete stranger, anyway.

Reyes left us soon after that, saying there wasn't much else he could add at that time. As soon as he was out of earshot, I brought up the subject of Orin and his knife. Justine and Clara both agreed I had made the right decision not to say anything.

"We have no reason to suspect him at this time, other than the fact he's kind of shady," Clara said. "I'm sure there were other shoppers here this morning, and until Reyes asks for a list of them, we don't need to mention Orin."

There wasn't anything else we were going to learn standing around in the parking lot, so I said goodbye to Justine and Clara and headed back to my apartment. I was so busy thinking about Mrs. Knowles that I forgot to go to the grocery store, but it hardly mattered. I had lost my appetite, anyway.

I only lasted about twenty minutes in my apartment before I grabbed my keys and went out for a walk. It didn't stop my brain from racing at full speed, but it was better than pacing back and forth in my little efficiency apartment.

Had I made a mistake by not telling Reyes about Orin? Like Clara had said, even though Orin was involved with the Dire Market, that didn't mean he was a killer. And, again, I could see no reason why he would have murdered

Mrs. Knowles. Between his diamond ring and however much money Damien had given him as an advance, I didn't think Orin had killed because he wanted to get the knife but couldn't pay for it.

So, what other reason might he have had, then? I came up with a lot of ridiculous scenarios, and none of them were plausible.

Still, though, I really wanted to get a look at Orin's knife. If it was the murder weapon, then there was a chance he hadn't cleaned it thoroughly. There could be evidence strapped to his thigh right at that moment.

I arrived at work that night about half an hour early. I had walked to the Sanctuary, though I was too busy thinking about the murder to appreciate the crisp air and the way the fluffy white clouds on the horizon were turning a brilliant shade of pink as the sun sank.

Orin might have been staying at the Sanctuary, but if he was, I had no idea which guest room he might be in. Besides, I wasn't sure I wanted to show up at his door and confront him one-on-one, anyway. I decided to start in the dining room, but as soon as I walked in, I knew he wasn't there, because Fiona was. She was just coming out of the kitchen, balancing two plates of food.

"Taking dinner up to Seraphina?" I asked in greeting.

"Yeah. She'll be down here for the family meeting, but she's hiding out as much as she can to avoid any chance encounters."

I inhaled deeply. "It smells delicious. And, believe it or not, I *am* hoping for a chance encounter. I want to get a look at Orin's knife, in case there's evidence he killed someone with it this morning."

Wordlessly, Fiona swept past me and put the plates down on the nearest table. She took me by the shoulders and guided me to the bench. "Justine told me about the owner of the antique store, but you think Orin might have done it?" she asked as we both sat down.

"He has a silver knife that he said he bought there this morning, on his way into Nightmare. I'm surprised Justine didn't mention my theory to you."

Fiona shrugged dismissively. "If it's just a theory, then I'm guessing she didn't tell me because she doesn't want me any more worried than I already am."

"Orin saw Mrs. Knowles today," I continued. "The question is whether or not she was still alive when he left the antique store. I think your death premonition was about Mrs. Knowles, and her connection to the Sanctuary was through Orin."

Fiona shook her head firmly, but I noticed the sliver of a smile on her face. "When I get the flash, it's for an inevitable death. Orin hadn't even met Mrs. Knowles when I got the flash last night, so that can't be our connection."

"Then why are you smiling?" I asked.

"Because," Fiona said, "last night, we were asking people here if their loved ones were okay, but we forgot to check in with two of our residents: Tanner and McCrory."

CHAPTER SEVEN

I pressed the palm of my hand to my forehead and groaned. "Of course! I should have realized it earlier. The ghosts used to live at the antique store!"

Fiona nodded. "Baxter found the box containing their six-shooters at that store. He realized Tanner and McCrory were tethered to it, so he bought the box and moved the ghosts into their new home here."

How that connection had escaped me earlier in the day was beyond me, and the only excuse I could come up with was that I had been so focused on Orin, I had completely forgotten the Sanctuary's true connection to Mining Town Antiques. Butch Tanner and Connor McCrory—the legendary Wild West outlaw and one of Nightmare's former sheriffs—had famously killed each other in a shootout on High Noon Boulevard. Their ghosts had been trapped on this plane since that fateful day in the late eighteen hundreds, tied to the guns they had used in the shootout.

"I'll have a chat with the ghosts," I said eagerly.

"Meanwhile, I'm taking dinner upstairs while it's still hot." Fiona stood and grabbed the plates, and as she headed for the door, she called over her shoulder, "Let us know what you find out!"

I was on Fiona's heels, until we took our separate paths in the entryway. She headed upstairs while I turned in the direction of Damien's office. I was so excited about talking to Tanner and McCrory that I didn't even stop to fill Damien in when I rushed into his office.

Damien had been sitting at his desk, but he stood abruptly. "Is there a problem?" he asked. He looked like he was ready to spring into action. Apparently, my energy was giving off emergency vibes rather than excited ones.

"Not at all! You'll know everything in a minute." Even as I was talking, I was moving past Damien and reaching toward the former hospital's old-fashioned call system. There was a panel on the wall behind the desk, filled with worn, tarnished brass buttons. Faded handwritten labels next to them told who each button could be used to call.

I pressed the button labeled *Tanner and McCrory* in what I now recognized as Baxter's spidery script. As I waited for the ghosts to arrive, I turned to Damien. "How does it work, anyway? The ghosts roam all over the building, so how do they hear when I call?"

"My father rigged up a special call for them. Instead of connecting to a bell, like the others, their button triggers a frequency only the ghosts can—" Damien stopped short as the ghosts floated down through the ceiling right next to me, landing on the carpet silently.

"Mister Damien, Miss Olivia," McCrory said, tipping his black cowboy hat toward us. I always thought McCrory looked more like a villain than a sheriff, since he wore a black suit, hat, and duster.

Tanner gave us a nod, his eyes glinting above the red bandana he wore over his mouth and nose. "Good evening."

"Now that the formalities are out of the way," McCrory said, crossing his arms, "why don't you tell us what you want? There's something strange going on here, but the two of us haven't quite figured it out. It has to do with our new guest though, doesn't it?"

Damien waved a hand toward me. "Olivia is the one who can answer that. I'm as lost as the two of you."

"Wait," Tanner instructed me. "Can you let me enjoy this moment a bit longer? The bossman is as ignorant as us! How about that, Sheriff?"

Damien made a noise that implied he was the most long-suffering boss of all time.

"Actually," I said, "I have some bad news for you two, if you haven't heard already. A friend of yours was murdered this morning. Mrs. Knowles, the owner of the antique store where you used to live."

Tanner and McCrory both stared at me silently. I was wondering if ghosts were capable of crying when Tanner snorted. McCrory's lip began to twitch.

"My condolences," I added.

To my utter surprise, both of the ghosts threw back their heads and started to laugh. They were practically guffawing, and Tanner clutched at his stomach as he leaned forward and bent nearly double.

"You think it's funny?" I asked, horrified.

"You would, too, if you had known her," McCrory said as his laughter began to taper off. He reached up and wiped at his cheek, which was either a habit from when he was alive or proof that ghosts could, in fact, cry.

"That old bat! I knew it was only a matter of time." Tanner straightened up and chuckled contentedly.

"Can you take us there later?" McCrory asked. "If we're lucky, then she's haunting the place now, and we can give her a not-so-warm welcome to the afterlife."

My face must have shown how astonished I was by the ghosts' complete lack of sympathy because Tanner gave a little shake of his head. "I know it's not the reaction you were expecting, Miss Olivia. But she wasn't a nice lady. At all."

I thought of what Justine had said about Mrs. Knowles and how she had always acted like Justine was beneath her. To Mrs. Knowles, Justine had been just another freak from the Sanctuary, a feeling so many other people in Nightmare seemed to have, too. But that didn't mean all the people who felt that way were bad, despite their misconceptions, so what made Mrs. Knowles an exception?

Damien seemed to be reading my mind because he asked, "What did she do that was so awful?"

"You two have a seat," McCrory said. "This might take a while."

Damien and I complied, and the ghosts took up a spot to one side of Damien's desk. Tanner even had his hands clasped behind his back, looking for all the world like he was about to give a presentation for school.

"Mrs. Knowles doesn't like anyone, and no one likes her," Tanner began.

"Liked. Past tense," McCrory corrected gleefully. "She's dead now."

"Even her husband disliked her. She judged everyone who came through the door of that store, and if she didn't think you were worthy of owning one of her precious antiques, then she wouldn't sell to you. She'd say an item was on hold for someone else, or she would claim the price tag was wrong and name some sky-high price no one in their right mind would pay."

"How did she stay in business?" I asked.

"She approved of enough folks that there was never a lack of customers," McCrory said. "Lots of tourists, mostly. Folks with enough money to be traveling."

"Mrs. Knowles didn't like us, either." Tanner sounded amused by that.

"She knew you were there?" Damien asked, surprised.

"Sure," Tanner drawled. "She saw us a few times. She had no idea we were tethered to our guns. She thought we were just ordinary ghosts who haunted the building."

"For that matter," McCrory broke in, "she didn't know those guns had belonged to a couple of famous people like us. She could have made a small fortune from our six-shooters, but Baxter got the guns—and us—for a hundred dollars. Of course, in my time, that *was* a fortune."

"Anyway," Tanner said pointedly, seeming annoyed that McCrory was interrupting his story, "Mrs. Knowles seemed to think we were some kind of troublemakers. Any time she glimpsed us out of the corner of her eye, she'd start shouting that she was going to call the local priest to come out and exercise us."

"Exorcise," McCrory corrected.

"That's what I said! So, we learned to lay low and not come out of hiding until she had gone home for the day. Baxter couldn't see us when he came in and picked up our six-shooter box, but he somehow felt us. He asked us to tell him our story, and we whispered it real quiet-like into his ear, so Mrs. Knowles wouldn't overhear. When we were done, Baxter said he could take us somewhere we would be safe. Somewhere we could come out anytime we wanted to, and no one would be scared. We said that would be great, and we've been here ever since."

I had to smile at that last part of the story. Baxter had carefully built the Sanctuary into a safe haven for supernatural creatures, and it had been kind of him to give the ghosts the choice between staying where they were and having a new home.

"There might have been a lot of people who disliked Mrs. Knowles," I said, "but who would have wanted her dead? You said even her husband disliked her. Could he have murdered her?"

Again, Tanner and McCrory laughed heartily.

"Oh, it's not going to be that easy," McCrory said. "The list of people who might have wanted her dead is a lot longer than that!"

CHAPTER EIGHT

My ears perked up at that. "Oh? Like who?"

"Like we said, she was mean to everyone," McCrory said. "Our dislike of Mrs. Knowles went beyond her threats to us. It was awful to see the way she treated people, day in and day out. Every time she hired a new employee, we'd take bets about how long they would last. I think the best we ever saw was a guy who stuck it out for eight whole months."

"And then there was the rumor about the store not really belonging to her," Tanner said. "I don't know the details, but I remember hearing bits of conversations. Someone was accusing Mrs. Knowles of not being the rightful owner, and that mess was still going on when we moved out."

It had been several decades since Tanner and McCrory had "moved out," but I knew how disputes like that could drag on. It was definitely something worth looking into.

"Talk to the husband," McCrory suggested, "but don't stop there. You need to talk to Mrs. Knowles's sister, as well. Sometimes they got along great, sometimes not."

"Oh!" Tanner said excitedly. "And you should talk to that one lady who worked there. Who knows? Maybe she still works there. The one with the frown and the orange hair."

"You just said employees came and went like that place was a revolving door," I pointed out.

Tanner and McCrory stared at me blankly. "It's a phrase," I clarified. "If employees don't last long there, what makes you think this one would still be around?"

"This wasn't long ago," Tanner said. "Just a short while before Baxter disappeared, he took us there with him. He thought it would be a fun outing for us."

"Never trust a lady with an unnatural hair color," McCrory mumbled. "I once met a gal with the brightest red hair you ever saw. By the end of the night, she'd taken every penny I had."

"Sounds like quite a night," Damien quipped.

Tanner whooped with laughter. "The sheriff got swindled by a lady!"

"I did not get swindled, thank you very much," McCrory said defensively.

"Thank you both for your help," I said, raising my voice to be heard over the brewing argument. "I'll call if I need any more information."

Tanner and McCrory disappeared through the wall between Damien's office and the hallway, still arguing about the redhead.

"I don't like it," Damien said as soon as it was just the two of us. "Orin showed up on the same day as a murder, and Justine told me he bought a knife at the antique store just this morning."

I was about to tell Damien that, according to Fiona, it couldn't have been Orin, but he kept talking as his shoulders slumped and he stared down at his desk. "What have I done? Am I being irresponsible by letting Orin stay in Nightmare? My father would have never let someone like him set foot inside the Sanctuary, let alone work for us."

"Your father is the reason Orin is here," I said. "Besides, I was about to tell you Orin isn't the killer."

That got Damien to look at me. "What makes you so sure?"

"Fiona." I relayed what she had told me about the timing of her flash that someone was going to die compared to when Orin had arrived in Nightmare.

Damien looked slightly comforted by that news, but he was chewing his lip as he stood. He seemed deep in thought, and he restlessly unbuttoned the jacket of his blue pinstripe suit and slid out of it before throwing it carelessly across the back of his chair. His white button-down shirt fit his muscular torso well, and I felt my heart give a little lurch.

How does he do that to me? I'm too old to get flustered by a nice physique.

"Can you help me know for certain that Orin isn't a suspect?" Damien finally asked me. "I hate to ask such a big favor, but I also know how much you enjoy poking your nose into murders."

I was glad to hear a hint of teasing in Damien's voice. That meant, whatever he might be feeling about Orin's ominous presence, he wasn't spiraling down into an emotional state that would have him chucking books around the room with his mind.

"Of course I'll look into it," I promised Damien. "I want to find the killer so I can yell at them about making me and my friends see such an awful sight."

Damien nodded. "Justine told me it was gruesome. I'm sorry you had to be the one who found her."

"Just my luck, right?" The clock on the mantel of the fireplace chimed just then, and I jumped. "It's time for the family meeting already? Okay, I'll keep you posted on anything I find out. See you later."

I hustled out of Damien's office, then slid onto a bench in the dining room just in time to hear Justine say I was going to be posted in the lagoon vignette again that night.

Typically, I took tickets at the front door more often than I was inside the haunt itself, and I had to wonder if this assignment was more about helping to keep an eye on Seraphina than it was about scaring guests as they came through.

I was happy to do both.

Once the meeting was over, I got changed into my pirate costume in a hurry. If I was going to be an informal part of Seraphina's security detail that night, then I didn't want to waste a moment. It had taken me a long time to learn my way through the dark, narrow pathways built between the various vignettes inside the haunt—we called them tunnels because that was really what they felt like—but I had become so familiar with the path from the east wing of the Sanctuary to the lagoon vignette that I could navigate it without thinking.

Soon, I was standing on the raised wooden walkway in the lagoon vignette. The floor below had been decorated to look like the boardwalk was crossing a real lagoon, and there were some actual pools of water to enhance the effect. A pirate ship loomed up on one side of the room to complete the look.

I had been so quick to get to my post that Seraphina hadn't even arrived yet. Soon, she appeared in the doorway. Theo was pushing her water tank.

"You doing okay, Seraphina?" I asked. She was sitting low in the tank, only the top half of her face visible.

Seraphina rose a few inches and scanned the room. With the overhead lights on, the entire vignette was easy to see, even with the fake moss and vines trailing down from well-hidden support beams. "Yeah. I'm hanging in there," she said distantly.

I had never seen Seraphina transfer between her mobile water tank and the big one that sat next to the pirate ship. Since the big tank was at least seven feet tall, I knew it wasn't as easy as jumping from one body of water to the other.

As I watched, Theo walked to the pirate ship and opened a small door built into its side. I had never even noticed the door before because it was so cleverly designed.

A moment later, Theo emerged on the deck of the pirate ship. I grinned at the sight. He was in his costume, his tricorn hat sitting jauntily on his head, and his zombie makeup looking especially gross in the bright lights. Theo really had been a pirate, albeit a vampire pirate rather than a zombie. Since he didn't have fangs anymore, he had chosen to pose as a zombie each night to look scarier. It was a shame, really: Theo was handsome under all that fake rotting skin.

Theo grabbed a rope that looked like part of the ship's rigging, and I saw it had a loop at one end. He deftly swung it over the side of the ship, in Seraphina's direction. She caught it, then slid the loop over her head and secured it underneath her arms. "Ready," she called up.

There must have been a hidden winch on the mast of the ship because there was a low humming noise as the rope pulled taut. Seraphina was lifted right out of her mobile tank, and Theo guided the rope toward the big tank. Once she was dangled over it, the rope began to lower.

"Neat," I commented. The mechanism was simple, and it looked like just another part of the pirate ship when Seraphina wasn't flying through the air with it.

"You'll be safe tonight," Theo called down after he had secured the rope to the mast again. "Try to have some fun, okay?"

It was good advice for all of us. I knew everyone would be hypervigilant as long as Orin was hanging around the Sanctuary, but if he was going to make a move to get Seraphina back in his possession, it certainly wasn't going to happen while she was in the vignette with us.

Theo came up to me before we opened for the night. It was odd to see a zombie looking concerned. "Malcolm is also on security detail tonight, so if you spot anyone lurking in the shadows, it's just him."

It wouldn't be the first time Malcolm had hidden himself in the crevice between the pirate ship and the back wall of the vignette, and I reminded myself not to jump if he suddenly emerged. "Got it," I assured Theo. "And I'll be keeping a close eye on Seraphina, too."

"Thanks." Theo bent forward and kissed my cheek, and I made a noise of disgust. He only ever did that when he had his zombie makeup on, and I knew he did it solely for my reaction.

It was easy to tell myself to let go of worry about Orin and Seraphina while the overhead lights were on. Once they clicked off, though, I felt tension snaking its way into my shoulders. I tried to distract myself by focusing all of my attention and energy on the guests as they began to trickle through the haunt. Thursday nights weren't our busiest, but they were a nice warm-up to the weekend crowds. And, compared to the night before, when the storm had kept people at home, the Sanctuary felt positively packed.

I made someone scream and cover their face in fear only ten minutes after we had opened. Apparently, I had found a good outlet for my nerves. Even still, I caught myself peering into every face that went past, wondering if Orin would hide himself among them.

Maybe that was why I seemed especially frightening that night. I was staring at each guest like they might be a murderer.

When it was time for my break, I went only after finding Malcolm in the shadows, so I knew Seraphina was well-guarded. Once I got to the dining room, I sat and ate my cookies and chips with my face toward the doors. I told myself I had no reason to be afraid of Orin, at least not for my own sake, but I also figured there was no reason not to take precautions.

I had relaxed a bit during my break, and we got through the rest of the night with no incidents. By the time the overhead lights turned on again at midnight, I had even managed to have a little fun.

I stuck around to watch Seraphina transfer back into her mobile water tank. When Malcolm and Theo escorted her out of the vignette, I followed, breaking off to head to the costume room so I could change clothes and go home.

Once I had my jeans, Nightmare Sanctuary T-shirt, and jacket on again, I headed out, calling goodnight to everyone I passed along the way to the front doors. The temperature outside had dipped dramatically, and I inhaled sharply when I opened one of the doors and walked out into the night air. I tucked my chin against the collar of my jacket and stuffed my hands into the pockets.

I had only taken one step when I caught a flicker of movement out of the corner of my eye. The voice coming from the direction of the shadows by the ticket window was male.

"I've been looking for you."

CHAPTER NINE

I screamed and jumped backward, hitting the door behind me. "Ow!" I yelped. Then, immediately after that, I felt more embarrassed than scared. Theo had told me at the start of the night that Malcolm would be lurking in the shadows and that I shouldn't let him startle me.

"Oh, dear, are you hurt?" Malcolm asked. He finally stepped out into the light of the portico's fixture high above us. The old chandelier swung in the breeze, sending shadows dancing across Malcolm's face.

I winced. "No, I'm okay. I feel silly more than anything."

"I didn't mean to scare you. I was waiting for you to get changed out of your costume so I can escort you home. It's a dangerous world out there."

I raised an eyebrow at Malcolm. "Are you walking me home because of the murder, or because of the Sanctuary's new guest?"

"Both." Malcolm lifted his top hat, revealing his bald head underneath, and gave me a small bow before offering his arm to me. "Shall we?"

I gladly took Malcolm's arm. Since I was jumping at shadows, it would be nice to have his company. Cowboy's Corral was about a mile away, down a dark side road with little traffic at that time of night. Ordinarily, I found it peaceful. Given the day's events, the route seemed almost dangerous. Anything could be lurking in the shadows, just like Malcolm had been.

We had made it along the entire length of the narrow dirt lane that linked the Sanctuary and the road before Malcolm paused and turned to me. The moon was half-full, illuminating the old gallows at the crossroads, and the night wind lifted the hem of Malcolm's long black coat. I felt like I was inside a scene from a gothic horror novel.

"You can't trust anyone who works on the Dire Market," Malcolm said in a low voice. I got the distinct impression he had waited to say that so there was no chance he'd be overheard by someone at the Sanctuary. And that someone, of course, was Orin. "What he did to Seraphina tells us he's not a good man."

I shivered, partly from the cold and partly from fear. "If he wasn't helping us track down Baxter, I'd think he was the villain in the story."

"He can be both a villain and a hero. He's helping us, yes, but for a price. This is just a job to him." Malcolm began walking again, his eyes looking up at the cloudless sky. "There are all types of supernatural creatures in this world, Olivia. Some of them are good, and some of them aren't. And then there are the ones like me."

"And what are you?" I asked. I had always thought Malcolm was one of the good guys.

"Reformed." Malcolm gave a low chuckle. "You know, I remember what the night sky looked like back when Nightmare was a thriving mining town. The population was much larger back then, but since there was no electricity, nighttime was truly dark. You could see so many stars."

"Do you miss it? Those old days, before cars, and the internet, and being able to cross the country in only a few hours?"

Malcolm laughed again, but it was a lot louder this

time. "You have no idea how bad this town smelled back then! All the horses, and thousands of sweaty miners. That was a true horror."

I laughed along with Malcom, and I forgot my fear for the rest of the walk back to my apartment.

After I said good night to Malcolm, I wasn't at all worried about him being alone as he returned to the Sanctuary. If Orin—or anyone, for that matter—tried to cross him, they would quickly learn they were outmatched. Wendigos were ferocious and fast, and their senses were primed for hunting humans.

As soon as I was alone in my apartment, I felt my fear growing again. I reminded myself, over and over, that even if Orin was dangerous, he had no reason to come after me. I was safe. Still, it took a while for me to drift off.

When I woke up on Friday morning, I got ready for the day and drank my first cup of coffee, then took my second cup with me to the motel office. Spending time with Mama always made me feel better. The walk between my apartment, which was in the right rear corner of the motel, and the office up front was a short one, but the air was brisk. A cold front must have blown in overnight.

I found Mama fiddling with the thermostat on one wall when I walked through the door of the office. "Stupid heater wasn't working this morning," she told me as she turned to see who had come through the front door. "Benny got it fixed, but it's having a tough time chasing the chill out of this place."

A cup of steaming coffee, I realized, could double as a tiny space heater. I wrapped my fingers around the mug. "I'm happy to report the one in my apartment works great."

"Good. One less thing to worry about, since you've got another murder on your hands."

I was mid-sip, and I nearly choked on my coffee as I

started to laugh. "Of course you've already heard about Mrs. Knowles."

"You and Luis must be best friends by now."

"I'm pretty sure Officer Reyes would be happy if I moved out of Nightmare and never came back."

Mama gave me a sly look. "You want to hear some gossip related to the victim?"

I leaned against the check-in counter. "Yes, please."

"Mrs. Knowles has a younger sister," Mama began, raising an eyebrow. She was clearly relishing the chance to give me the scoop. "Tina showed up at the antique store yesterday afternoon, just hours after her sister's body had been carted away. She demanded the police turn the antique store's keys over to her."

"Is Tina more concerned about selling antiques than about her own sister's murder?"

"Great question. When the police told Tina they couldn't do that, because Mr. Knowles was now the rightful owner of the store, things got so heated that one of the officers threatened to arrest Tina."

"She really wants her sister's store. Did she want it badly enough to kill for it?" I didn't feel silly for asking the question, because Mama seemed to be implying it was a possibility.

"Tina didn't appear to be grieving, that's for sure," Mama said.

"Of course," I speculated, "she might have been in shock."

"Maybe. I heard the news when I stopped into the bakery this morning. One of the gals in line ahead of me works at the police station, and she was filling us in. Oh, speaking of, would you like a cinnamon roll?" Mama went behind the counter and lifted a white pastry box onto it. She didn't have to ask me twice, and I eagerly grabbed a roll and bit into it.

"I wonder why Tina thinks she should get the keys to the store?" I mused as soon as I had swallowed.

"She told the police the place is legally hers, and that Mr. Knowles has no claim to it. According to the gossip from the bakery, Tina said, and I quote, 'Read the will.'"

"Interesting. Tanner and McCrory mentioned that no one liked Mrs. Knowles, including her own husband. If she left the store to her sister instead of to him, that could be one of the reasons."

"I guess we'll find out when the family meets with their lawyer."

I chuckled. "Because of course whatever happens in that private meeting will be public information two hours later."

"In this town? I give it one hour."

"Did you know her?" I asked. "You must have, since you seem to know everyone in Nightmare."

"Only in passing. She wasn't as horrible to me as she was to other customers at the store, probably because she knew I deal with a lot of tourists here at the motel. I could either recommend her store or tell them to steer clear, so Mrs. Knowles wanted to keep me relatively happy."

I nibbled thoughtfully at my cinnamon roll. "Someone had to like the woman."

Mama shrugged. "She could turn on the charm when it suited her. I once saw her talk a man into selling his antique watch for at least half of what it was worth. She smiled and flirted with him, then handed the cash over like she'd done him a favor."

"There are plenty of suspects living here in Nightmare," I said thoughtfully.

"As opposed to living where?"

"Oh." I waved a hand. "There's a guy—a tooth fairy, believe it or not—staying at the Sanctuary right now. He's got some leads that might help us find Baxter, but I distrust him enough that he was the first person I thought of when we found Mrs. Knowles." I told Mama about Orin, and she could only shake her head and warn me to be careful.

Once I had finished my unexpected breakfast and gotten three more warnings about Orin, I thanked Mama for the gossip and went back to my apartment to get some work done. I did marketing for Cowboy's Corral in exchange for living there, and ordinarily, I would take my laptop to the office and work in one of the lobby chairs. Given the frigid temperature in the office, though, I opted for the warmth of my own apartment.

I was certain the antique store wouldn't be open, so there was no point trying to go there to learn anything new. Once it reopened, I could go look for the woman Tanner had referred to as the "orange-haired lady," and maybe I would get lucky and bump into the sister, too.

I gave up trying to work after an hour. My brain was more interested in the murder than in marketing, and I shut the lid of the laptop with a frustrated *bang*. Since I couldn't focus enough to get work done, and I didn't know what to do at the moment to learn more about the murder, I decided I should go ahead and go grocery shopping. Once again, if I wanted to have lunch, it would have to be done.

As I drove to the store, I realized about half of the license plates of the cars around me were from out of state. The winter really was our big tourist season, and visitors seemed to be descending on the city in droves. That was good because it meant the Sanctuary would probably be busy that night.

I was halfway to the grocery store when I realized the cars ahead of me were slowing down. We came to an absolute standstill for about three minutes, but I couldn't see what was going on ahead of us. When traffic did begin to move again, it was at a crawl, and everyone ahead of me was turning right.

When I made it to the front of the line, I could see three police cars ahead of me. They were parked across the road, blocking traffic, so we were being diverted onto a side road.

"I just want to get my grocery shopping done," I muttered. Yesterday, it had been a dead body standing in my way. Today, the road had been shut down.

But I did, eventually, get to the store. It took a bit of wandering around on side roads to get there, but I was finally driving a shopping cart instead of my car.

While I was checking out, I was thinking about the price of breakfast sausages rather than murder. The clerk behind the counter interrupted my thoughts as she scanned my diet soda.

"So," she said, looking up at me from underneath long eyelashes, "are you stocking up for the farewell party for Cynthia Knowles?"

CHAPTER TEN

"Party?" I repeated. Maybe the clerk had meant to say memorial, I thought.

"Oh, yeah. We're going to celebrate hard." She continued scanning my groceries, like having a party for a murdered woman was something that happened every Friday night.

"Was there anyone in this town who liked Mrs. Knowles?"

The girl, who was probably in her early twenties, waved my package of bagels in a little circle. "Not a single person. I worked at the antique store a few times, during busy season. She was the meanest old lady you ever met, and not just to those of us who worked there. She would insult customers even while she was running their credit cards."

"I never met her, but every report I hear makes her sound even worse."

The clerk laughed sharply. "You should hear Wanda's stories! She's been working there for a few years, and the party was her idea. We're grilling out at Pioneer Park tonight, and anyone who wants to celebrate the death of the meanest witch in Nightmare is welcome to join us. Just bring a side dish, please."

People were holding a potluck to celebrate a murder. I

was horrified, and I mumbled something about having to work that night. Then, in a clearer voice, I added, "Besides, aren't you worried about your safety? There's a killer in our town."

"What, are you a true crime junkie, or something? Somebody finally got sick enough of Mrs. Knowles to kill her. There's not a serial killer running around Nightmare."

Oh, honey, if you only knew the things that are running around this town.

I made a noncommittal noise, then added casually, "I wonder if I've met your friend who works there. Orange hair, right?"

The clerk laughed again. "Wanda's hair is green now. You're about four colors behind, so it's been a while since you saw her!"

"Enjoy your party," I said as I collected my groceries and left. Wanda was someone I'd want to have a chat with just as soon as the antique store was open again. And, as awful as I thought the party idea was, part of me wished I could be there so I could talk to potential suspects. Would a murderer throw a party to celebrate their success?

Maybe.

The police still had the road blocked as I drove home, and I wondered what could be going on that required diverting traffic plus three police cars. Maybe Mama would hear that bit of gossip before long, and she could fill me in.

I got home, put away my groceries, then stared into my fridge while I wondered what I wanted to make for lunch. After that chat with the clerk, my brain was buzzing again, and I couldn't make a decision.

My fingers were reaching for my cell phone almost before I realized what I was doing. I called Damien, and when he picked up, I said, "Do you want to practice a bit this afternoon?" The first answer I got was the sound of my stomach growling, so I added, "Or maybe grab a late lunch?"

Damien seemed surprised by that second suggestion. "Lunch? Oh, I can't do either, actually. I have a stupid Chamber of Commerce mixer I have to go to this afternoon, and I need to take care of a few things first."

"If it's stupid, then why are you bothering to go?"

I could just imagine the resigned look on Damien's face as he answered, "My father did all that stuff. He always thought it was important for the Sanctuary to show it was a part of the Nightmare community, and not just a bunch of weirdos on the outskirts of town. I'm trying to keep that up in his absence."

"It's the right thing to do," I consoled him. "Besides, I'm sure it won't be that bad. I'll see you tonight."

I was about to hang up when Damien said quickly, "Wait! Why don't you come with me? You're a marketing person, so you're good at making all that boring small talk."

"Gee, thanks."

"You know what I mean. Plus, even if I can't get any practice in, you can. What a great chance for you to work on your conjuring skills! Everyone will be talking about the murder, and maybe, if you focus, you can conjure some inside info about it."

That was a lot more enticing than the idea of making small talk with other Nightmare businesspeople, and I readily agreed. It sure beat sitting in my apartment, feeling restless. Damien said he would pick me up at two thirty, adding, "Meet me at the front office of the motel. Mama called and said I have to come by for a cinnamon roll."

By the time I needed to meet Damien, I had gotten dressed in what I figured passed for business casual in Nightmare. I had gotten rid of most of my professional wardrobe in the wake of my divorce and bankruptcy filing, selling off the designer pieces that could get me some quick cash. I didn't have a lot left in the way of nice clothes, but I felt like my houndstooth dress and a black cardigan made a nice combination. The dress had always hugged my curves nicely, and the neckline was cut just right to show off the necklace Damien had given me. Two tiny charms—a cross and a pentagram—hung from the silver chain.

I fingered the charms as I gave myself a last look in my bathroom mirror before heading to the motel office. Baxter had given the necklace to Lucille, who was Mama's sister and Damien's mother. Damien had then given it to me because it was warded with powerful protection spells, and he thought I had a knack for getting myself into trouble.

Hopefully, something as innocent as a Chamber of Commerce mixer wouldn't be a threat, but I always wore the necklace, just in case. I liked the idea of having some protective magic around me, plus I appreciated the fact that Damien had given me something so sentimental. It was one of the few things he had to remind him of his mother, who had ceased to exist in human form when he was a toddler. Lucille hadn't died, since there was no body. It was more like she had transformed into a spirit. In the past few months, she had started making her presence known to us, like she had lain dormant for more than forty years but was finally beginning to wake up.

I added a light black coat to my ensemble since the day wasn't getting any warmer, then went to the office. As soon as I walked in, Mama gave me a look of approval. "Oh, he's going to like that."

I felt warmth blooming in my cheeks. "Mama! I'm not dressed like this for Damien."

"I know. He told me you two are going to a Chamber of Commerce mixer, and I'm sure you put on that dress so you'd look good for all the complete strangers who will be there for the free beer."

"No. That's not... I didn't…" I stopped myself and took a measured breath. "I put this on because I feel good in it. I hardly ever have a chance to dress up since I came to Nightmare, and I'm taking advantage of this opportunity."

"Hmm." Mama just looked at me with a small smile. She was utterly determined to set me up with Damien, and the more I resisted, the harder she tried.

When the bell above the door sounded a moment later, I purposely kept my face turned in the direction of the back wall. I didn't want to look at Damien while my cheeks were still blazing.

I was surprised, then, when I heard several quick, light footsteps, and arms suddenly wrapped around my waist. I looked down to find Mama's granddaughter, Lucy. Her face was pressed against my side, and all I could see was her mass of brown curls.

"Hi, Lucy!" I said happily, my embarrassment forgotten. "It's good to see you, too!"

"Hey, Miss Olivia!" Lucy stepped back and thrust her arm toward my face. "Look at my new bracelet! My friend Krista gave it to me at school today."

I admired Lucy's beaded bracelet even as I heard Mama's voice in the background. "You look like you've seen a ghost," she said.

I looked up and saw she was addressing her son, Nick. Usually, Nick had a wide smile on his tanned face. His eyes were blue, like his mom's, and there was always a feeling of warmth and friendliness in Nick's demeanor. Right then, though, Mama was right. His face was pale and slightly slack, and there was a dullness in his eyes.

"I just picked up Lucy at school," Nick said quietly. He glanced significantly toward his daughter.

"Lucy, dear, can you do me a big favor?" Mama asked in a voice dripping with sweetness. "There's a box of brochures upstairs for the horseback riding tours. Can you please go get it for me?"

"Sure, Grandma!" Lucy bounded up the stairs.

Nick gave me a nod as I joined him and Mama. We stood closely together so there was no way Lucy could overhear Nick as he explained, "The police were just reopening the road when I was on my way to the elementary school. While I was waiting for Lucy, one of the other parents came over to tell me why it had been closed off in the first place."

Nick glanced toward the stairs, then looked between Mama and me before he continued. "The police found the murder weapon in an overgrown area just off the road. Mrs. Knowles was killed with an axe."

CHAPTER ELEVEN

"So that's why there were three police cars blocking the road," I said. "How did someone happen to find the murder weapon along that stretch? It's all so wild and overgrown."

"But there's a trail back there," Nick said. "It parallels the road, but it's set back far enough that you've probably never noticed it behind all the scrubby little bushes and Palo Verde trees. A volunteer group was doing a trail cleanup this morning, picking up trash, and someone noticed something glinting in the underbrush."

"And it was an axe," Mama said in a shocked tone. "What an awful discovery."

"Yes, but this will be enormously helpful for the police," Nick countered. "They speculate someone grabbed it off a shelf at the antique store, killed Mrs. Knowles, then fled the scene. The killer probably threw it from their car as they drove past an overgrown area, thinking it would never be found."

I was having a lot of thoughts on the news, but before I could say anything, two things happened at once. Lucy came bounding down the stairs at the same time Damien walked through the front door.

"Mister Damien!" Lucy shouted. She chucked the box

of brochures onto the floor and rushed toward him, her arms outstretched.

"How's my favorite pirate?" Damien asked as he swept Lucy up in a hug.

"I have to do my science fair project this weekend," Lucy said with a huff. "Real pirates don't have to do science fair projects."

"Pirates used science all the time," Damien countered. "They used the stars to help them navigate, and they knew how to preserve food so it wouldn't go bad while they were at sea for weeks at a time, and—"

Damien cut off as Lucy gasped loudly. "My project is about beef jerky, and why it doesn't go bad as fast as regular meat! I really am a pirate!"

Even Nick, as shaken as he seemed about the discovery of the axe, had to laugh at that.

Mama quickly found an excuse to send Lucy upstairs again, so Nick could fill Damien in on the news. When Nick was finished, Damien gave me a significant look. "So, she wasn't killed with a knife, then?"

"Not a knife," I confirmed. "That's another point in Orin's favor."

"The husband and the sister seem to be the most likely suspects," Damien noted.

"And the green-haired girl," I said.

"I thought it was orange hair?"

"It was, but it's green now. Her name is Wanda, she still works at the antique store, and she's helping throw a party tonight to celebrate the demise of Mrs. Knowles."

"Who's got the hot gossip now?" Mama sounded impressed.

I shrugged. "I had a very interesting conversation with the clerk at the grocery store today. It was possibly the most productive shopping trip I've ever had."

"With your social skills, I should make you go to every

Chamber of Commerce event with me." Damien beamed at me, his smile looking both proud and teasing. His smile faded, and he added, "The husband, the sister, and the green-haired employee are our suspects, then."

"Correct. That's good news for us."

Mama and Nick were watching our exchange, and Nick said, "How is that good news?"

"We have a guest staying at the Sanctuary right now," Damien said. "Orin's arrival in Nightmare and the murder happened around the same time, so we were feeling suspicious."

"Olivia filled me in on your *guest*," Mama told Damien, putting emphasis on the last word. Nick didn't know about the supernatural world, and I wasn't sure if she was trying to warn us not to spill the beans or questioning Damien's judgment for allowing Orin to stay at the Sanctuary. "If you thought him capable of murder, then hopefully he gets his business in Nightmare wrapped up quickly."

"Agreed," Damien said. "Meanwhile, Olivia and I have to go be good, involved members of the Nightmare business community."

Mama laughed. "Have fun! I'd normally be there, but I've got to mind the office while Benny finishes getting all the heaters working in the rooms."

Soon, I was in the passenger seat of Damien's silver Corvette. I expressed my relief that not only was the murder weapon an axe rather than a knife, but Orin had gone to the antique store after Fiona's flash.

"I still don't like Orin," Damien agreed, "but at least now we don't have to wonder if he killed an old lady yesterday."

We drove in silence for a few minutes before Damien said in a neutral tone, "You look nice today."

I glanced over at him, but his eyes were hidden behind his mirrored sunglasses. "Thanks," I said, reaching down to smooth my dress self-consciously. For the second time, the attention I was getting in it was making me feel a little embarrassed.

When did I forget how to take a compliment?

The first stretch of silence had been a comfortable one, but I could tell the looming silence after Damien's comment was going to be the awkward kind, so I looked for anything I could say to hold it at bay. "I'll focus on wanting to learn more about the murder," I said abruptly. "I'll be trying my hardest to conjure clues."

"And I'll be trying my hardest to act interested in things like the upcoming arts and crafts festival."

"Ooh, when is that?"

Damien glanced at me, and he seemed uncertain whether I was being sarcastic or not. "Sometime next month."

"That will be fun." When Damien gave me another sidelong glance, I said, "I mean it! I love a good arts festival. Pretty things to look at, lots of fresh air and sunshine, and fried food. What's not to love?"

Damien didn't answer, but I got the impression he felt there was a lot not to love about an arts and crafts festival. "Watch out," I warned teasingly, "or you're going to take Zach's spot as King of the Grumps."

"Sorry. It's just this whole thing with Orin. He's costing me a lot of stress and money."

I began to reach toward Damien and realized the only available real estate on him was his thigh. I pulled my hand back and said, "He won't be here for long. We'll get through this."

We began to slow, and Damien turned into the parking lot of Spaghetti Western. It was Nightmare's Italian restaurant, and I instantly felt more excited about having to attend the mixer. I didn't care how many businesspeople I had to make small talk with, if it meant I got to have a few meatballs.

There was a banquet room at the back of the restaurant, and the tables had been removed to give everyone from the Chamber of Commerce a place to mingle. There was a long table full of finger foods along one wall and a smaller table with a selection of drinks on it. A bored-looking bartender was busy making cocktails.

I made a beeline for the meatballs. Once I had a few of those in my belly, I felt ready to work my way through the room. Damien had already drifted away from me, and I saw him standing in one corner, chatting with an older man in a nice suit.

Leave it to Damien to find the one other person here dressed as nicely as he is.

I got a diet soda and scanned the room, focusing all my intent on learning more about the murder. *Who killed Mrs. Knowles?* I thought. *I am going to get a clue right here, right now.*

Instead, what I got was a knock to the shoulder.

"Oh, I'm so sorry!" The man who had run into me patted the spot on my shoulder, and I could smell alcohol on his breath. "Are you okay?"

"I'm fine."

"I was keeping an eye out for the mayor, and I just walked right into you." The man was wearing an expensive-looking blue-and-white-striped shirt with blue trousers, and his brown loafers looked freshly shined. "We haven't met. I'm Wally Hart."

"Olivia Kendrick," I said, shaking his proffered hand. Wally looked like he was in his early fifties, if his lined forehead and the gray at his temples were any indication. He was a nice-looking man—what my mother would have called "well put together." Wally even had gold cufflinks.

Wally reached past me and grabbed a glass of white wine from the drink station. He downed it in two gulps.

"Sorry," he said to me for the second time in less than a minute. "It's been a rough day."

"Oh, no. I hope it's nothing too bad?"

Wally plunked his glass down and motioned for the bartender to refill it. "I'm the lawyer for the Knowles family," he said grimly. "We had the reading of the will today. Cynthia isn't even in the ground yet, and all the family cares about is what they're going to get out of her death."

I nodded. "I've heard she wasn't very well liked." *I am going to get a clue right here, right now.* I was conjuring with all my might. "I also heard her sister, Tina, thought she had dibs on the antique store."

"That's because she does."

I fought to keep a neutral look on my face. "Really? I would have thought Mr. Knowles would be the new owner of the store."

Wally gulped down another glass of wine, then wiped the back of a hand across his mouth. He looked around furtively, then took a step closer to me. "I'm not supposed to say this, but I'm sure the news is already flying around town. Tina Denning had every right to claim she, as you say, had dibs on the store. Cynthia changed her will toward the end of last year to name Tina as the inheritor. Fred knew nothing about it. You should have seen his face when I read that clause in the will. I thought he was going to dive across the desk and murder me!"

CHAPTER TWELVE

Even as I told Wally I was happy to see he had not, after all, been strangled by an upset widower, I was wondering why in the world Cynthia had changed her will to give the store to her sister instead of her husband.

It sounded like Fred Knowles had no idea about the change, so did that mean he was no longer a suspect? No, I decided. If he had that kind of temper, then he was still on my list.

"Do you have any idea why Mrs. Knowles requested the change?" I asked as Wally brought a third glass of wine to his lips.

Wally tried to shake his head while he drank, and a little bit of wine spilled down his chin. As he wiped at it absently, he said, "Not a clue, but I have a feeling we're in for a long legal battle. Fred isn't going to take this lying down."

I frowned. "But it's a will that was legally changed. How can he argue against that?"

"Even if he doesn't think he can win, he can still make life a nightmare for Tina." Wally began to giggle. "A nightmare in Nightmare!"

Oh, boy, I really hope Wally has someone to drive him home after this.

Even as I was thinking that, Wally gave me a halfhearted wave. "I need to find something stronger than this. Nice meeting you."

Wally wandered off, and I practically sprinted toward Damien. He was still talking to the well-dressed gentleman, and I slowed my pace as I approached. I didn't want to seem rude.

Damien spotted me and waved me forward. "Buck, this is Olivia, she works with me at the Sanctuary. Olivia, Buck Olsen. He owns the car dealership about half a mile south of here."

"Oh!" I said, extending a hand as recognition set in. "I've seen your commercials on TV. Buck Olsen's best bet bargains!"

Buck laughed heartily, then gave me an exaggerated wink. "I paid a lot of money for that little jingle, but the fact that you remember it tells me it was worth every penny. Nice to meet you, Olivia. Now, if you'll excuse me, I see Wally Hart over there looking like he's about to fall over. I'm going to drive him home in one of those best bet bargains!"

Wow, did I just conjure a ride home for Wally, too?

Once Buck was out of earshot, I grabbed Damien's arm and steered him a little farther from the crowd. "It worked!" I hissed as loudly as I dared. "My conjuring worked!"

Damien grinned at me. "Of course it did! Your skills keep improving, Olivia. If you keep it up, you're going to be a very powerful conjuror before long."

The praise felt nice, even though I found myself making excuses. "Wally is really drunk, so I think a lot of it had to do with him being too inebriated to keep secrets."

"Wally gave you info? The lawyer?"

"Yeah, he works for the Knowles family. He said Cynthia Knowles changed her will late last year, leaving the antique store to her sister. Her husband, Fred, thought it was going to be his until the reading of the will today. Apparently, he was really upset."

"Understandable. Good work, Olivia."

"The wine did a lot of the work, too."

Damien looked at me seriously. "Stop doing that. Stop downplaying your abilities. You're amazing, Olivia, and at some point, you need to own it."

I was being lectured and praised at the same time, and Damien was looking at me so intently I thought I detected a hint of a glow in his eyes. His eyes only glowed when his emotions were heightened. Apparently, he *really* wanted me to embrace my talent for conjuring.

Suddenly, I smiled at Damien wickedly. "Have it your way. I was incredible back there, and I conjured like a boss!"

Damien put a hand over my shoulder and squeezed. "That's more like it! Now get back in there and do it again."

I tried. I talked to three people who were pleasant but not even interested in discussing the murder, and then I ran into Emmett Kline, the real estate agent. He and I had a nice time catching up with each other, but it was clear my conjuring wasn't working.

We had been there for more than an hour, and I knew we would be leaving soon, since Damien and I both had to be at the Sanctuary that night, and we had agreed on our way into the mixer that a little downtime before work would be nice.

I was spared from having to pick someone new to chat up by the approach of a man about my age, or maybe closer to his late forties. He was wearing a black polo shirt with *Nightmare Taxes* embroidered on it in yellow script.

"Because taxes are a nightmare to do, or because we're in Nightmare?" I asked even before he had a chance to introduce himself.

The man smiled. "Both. I'm Bryce Bonner. My accounting office is in the New Downtown."

I introduced myself and settled in for a talk about money and taxes, but Bryce surprised me by saying, "Town is buzzing with the news of this murder."

"It sure seems like it," I said, feeling my hope rise.

"My mother said it was no surprise someone finally got sick and tired of Mrs. Knowles. Between her being rude to any person she deemed unworthy and her ability to cheat anyone out of their valuable antiques, probably half this town had a reason to get rid of her."

Oh, so it's just going to be another one of those discussions. So much for conjuring a new clue. "I'm still trying to find the one person in Nightmare who actually liked Mrs. Knowles," I said.

"Good luck. I bet that by next month's mixer, you'll tell me your search is still on." Bryce glanced at someone behind me. "If you'll excuse me, I need to go say hello to the mayor."

Bryce bustled off, and I mentally patted myself on the back. I was still working on my conjuring skills, and I couldn't expect a one-hundred percent success rate this early into my supernatural journey. I had to celebrate my one win.

Damien was moving toward me, and I raised my eyebrows at him questioningly. He gave me a little nod, and we turned in unison to head out the door. During the drive back to my apartment, Damien spent half the time praising me, again, for my success with Wally Hart.

This time, I didn't protest that the alcohol had been the thing that had gotten Wally's tongue moving, rather than my conjuring. I let myself soak up the praise. It still felt awkward, but I told myself it was good to accept compliments without trying to brush them off.

I had a few hours before I needed to be at the Sanctuary for work that night, and after doing a little marketing work for the motel, I happily flopped into bed for a short nap. I drifted off while trying to decide if conjuring took more energy than I had realized.

Once I woke up, the first thing I did was stick my head out the front door to see what was happening with the weather. The temperature had dropped even more, which told me it was a night for the black Nightmare Sanctuary hoodie Justine had given me recently, rather than my usual T-shirt. It was cold enough that I opted to drive to work, too. I wanted to stay warm.

And, if I were being honest, I was still feeling a little on edge about wandering down dark roads by myself.

Usually, when I crossed the threshold into the Sanctuary, I felt a sort of lightness. That was the place where most of my friends lived, and I loved my job, so going there felt good. On that night, though, that feeling of warmth was missing. I felt almost nervous as I walked into the entryway.

I stopped and looked around, wondering what was giving me that feeling. There was no one else in the room, but there was a prickle on the back of my neck, like someone was watching me.

Without hesitation, I headed for Damien's office. His door was shut, which was unusual unless someone was in there with him, but I knocked, anyway. Instead of hearing him call for me to come in, I heard footsteps and the distinct *clack* of the lock being undone. When the door swung open, I simply said, "Something is wrong here."

Damien waved me inside and returned to his desk. "No, nothing is wrong," he said, as if he were unsure himself. "Everyone is on eggshells because of Orin."

"You locked your door so he couldn't sneak up on you," I guessed. "We know he wasn't the killer, though."

"But he's still the man who held Seraphina captive, and

he's a black-market dealer. There's a lot of information in this office I don't want him getting into." Damien pursed his lips. "Plus, he just gives all of us the heebie-jeebies."

I laughed at that, despite the tension I felt. "That makes it sound a little less ominous."

"If you can feel the tension here, then so will our guests tonight. They want to get scared, but in a fun way. So, if saying 'heebie-jeebies' makes you laugh, then it's a good thing. Try to spread a little bit of happiness tonight, okay?"

"I promise."

The mood in the dining room felt the same, and even the voices of everyone chatting before the start of the family meeting seemed subdued. I tried my best to make good on my promise to Damien, though, and when the conversation at my table turned to Orin, I interrupted with, "Did Damien tell you about my conjuring success today?"

Mori's eyes widened. "No! Fill us in!"

I did, and when I was done, Mori squeezed my arm and congratulated me while Theo whistled loudly. That got the attention of Malcolm, who was striding past us toward the front of the room. Soon, I had filled him in, as well.

Word must have spread from one table to the next, because when Justine stepped up to the podium, she opened with, "Apparently, Olivia took a big step forward in her conjuring abilities today." She gestured toward me and grinned. "She got some valuable information about the murder, from the victim's lawyer, no less!"

Everyone began to clap, and I heard a few cheers. Having all the attention on me was embarrassing but also gratifying. My friends were supporting me and celebrating my success. It was something I hadn't experienced a lot during my last couple of years in Nashville, and it felt wonderful to have such positive people in my life again.

And, to make it even better, the grim mood in the

room had dissipated by the time the applause died down and Justine moved on to other announcements. I would have to tell Damien that I had spread some happiness, and I had done it by owning my abilities rather than downplaying them. The news would make him doubly happy.

I was going to be at the front door that night, taking tickets. By the time I got up there shortly before opening, the temperature had dropped even further, and there was a bite in the breeze that made its way under the portico every now and then.

Thankfully, it was a Friday night, which meant there was a nonstop stream of people coming through the door. The crowd helped block some of the breeze, and I was so busy I didn't have much time to think about how icy the tip of my nose was.

I did have time to think about it during the last half hour of the night, when the line had dwindled to a trickle of people. I was rubbing my hands together briskly when two women walked up.

"It will be open tomorrow," one of them was saying. "They know everyone in town will want to shop there."

"They'll make a killing," said her companion. The two women snickered.

As I reached out to take the pair of tickets, I said, "Is there something happening tomorrow?"

The first woman nodded. "The antique store is reopening. Didn't you see the flyers that popped up all over town this afternoon?"

"No. I figured the store would be closed for a while yet."

The woman who had made the joke grinned. "They're having a sale. The flyer said, and I quote, 'All prices axed!'"

CHAPTER THIRTEEN

The two women began to laugh.

"You're joking," I said once they had quieted down enough to hear me.

They shook their heads and snickered again.

"Quite the marketing tactic," I mumbled as I tore their tickets and handed them back.

As the women went past me and joined the short queue inside the entryway, I realized the one had been absolutely right: everyone in Nightmare was going to want to go to the antique store. The murder there was the biggest news in town, and Nightmare residents loved getting as close to the gossip as possible. I could picture people trying to find the exact spot where the lifeless body of Mrs. Knowles had lain.

Yuck. Someone must have done a very quick but very thorough cleaning job.

The flyer's tagline was in terribly bad taste, and I wondered who was behind it. Had Tina Knowles made the flyers, hoping to begin her ownership of the store with a record sales day? Or, had it been the green-haired employee, Wanda, that was helping throw a party even at that very moment?

As disgusted as I was by someone using the murder to drum up business, I was also a little disgusted with myself.

Like everyone else, I also wanted to go to the antique store, partly out of sheer curiosity but also in the hope of learning more about the murder. Even though I told myself it hadn't been Orin who killed Mrs. Knowles, there was still a part of me that wasn't convinced.

So, as soon as the last guests had gone through the haunt and the Sanctuary closed for the night, I went in search of Justine and Clara. It only seemed right that they should be the ones to accompany me to the store.

I found both of them in the witches' forest vignette. Justine was lying on her back, with her head nearly underneath a giant black cauldron that looked like it was sitting on top of a real fire.

"Is it working now?" Justine called.

"Nope," Clara said. "Still no smoke."

Justine muttered something, and I could see her arms moving as her hands worked on something underneath the cauldron.

"Technical difficulties?" I asked as I walked up.

"The cauldron stopped smoking, so we thought we'd take a quick look," Clara explained.

As if in response, a puff of smoke rose from the cauldron. "How about now?" Justine asked.

"We've got smoke!" Clara cried happily.

Justine's head appeared, and she stood up and stretched. "The line got clogged. It seems to happen about every six months."

"Fancy going antique shopping tomorrow?" I asked the two of them.

Clara looked at me skeptically. "Surely Mining Town Antiques isn't going to be open."

"According to a couple of our guests tonight, flyers were posted all over town today announcing the store is having a sale tomorrow. 'All prices axed' was their exact quote."

"Oof," Justine said. "Bad taste."

"Too soon," Clara added.

"Agreed." I felt the corners of my mouth turn up. "So, do you want to go with me?"

"Obviously," Clara said as Justine nodded her head emphatically.

"I can pick you two up around noon," I suggested.

Justine and Clara quickly agreed, so I said good night to them. I retrieved my purse from the locker in the staff ladies' room, then headed toward the front doors. I was ready to get home and fall into bed.

I got halfway to the entryway when someone walked into the hallway, heading toward me. I was just opening my mouth to say good night to whichever of my co-workers it was when I realized it was Orin. He was wearing a brown leather coat that had dark stains on it, and his boots looked only slightly less dirty.

Just seeing him sent a stab of discomfort through me, but since this was the first time I had seen Orin since our introduction, I wanted to make the most of it. "Good evening, Orin," I said in as pleasant of a voice as I could manage.

"Hello, Conjuror," Orin answered. He seemed surprised I was talking to him, and I wondered if most of the people at the Sanctuary were simply pretending he wasn't there at all.

"Can I see your knife? The one you got at the antique store?"

I was utterly surprised when Orin pulled the knife out of the sheath on his thigh and handed it toward me hilt-first. I had expected him to say no. The knife was stunning. The mother-of-pearl hilt was smooth and shiny, with something carved along the edge that looked like Latin. The blade itself had a beautiful scrollwork design on it.

"Looking for traces of blood in case I killed that lady?"

Orin asked. He sounded deadly serious, and I jumped at his directness.

I took a moment to compose myself before I answered, "Mrs. Knowles wasn't killed with a knife. I was just curious about it, that's all. How do you know it's real silver?"

"I deal in this kind of stuff. I can tell." As I handed the knife back to Orin, he stepped so he was standing next to me, and he held the knife up to point at the scrollwork on the blade. "See these markings inside the design? They're like a user manual. That circle indicates a full moon, for werewolves. That lopsided triangle represents fairy wings."

My head swam as the reality of what Orin was saying set in. "This is a hunter's knife. It's made from silver so it can kill werewolves and fairies."

"Exactly. You have no idea the price something like this will fetch on the market. But, since I just got that nice paycheck from your boss, I don't need to sell it right now." Orin looked at the knife proudly, tilting it in his hand so it reflected the light. "In fact, I might never sell it. It's not every day you find a hunter's weapon out in the wild."

Out in the wild, I thought. *More like sitting on the shelf of an antique store whose owner was just murdered.*

"I wonder whose it was," I mused. I thought of Jeff Crosley, the owner of The Lusty Lunch Counter. He had once been a hunter, though these days his life was all about lunch specials and bottomless coffee. Maybe he had quietly sold some of his weapons since retiring from his first profession.

"And is the hunter who used to own this still alive?" Orin asked. There was a look in his eyes that said he might like to do something about that, using the very knife in his hand. With a resigned little sigh, he sheathed the knife. "A good hunter wouldn't be so easy to find, unfortunately."

I knew supernatural creatures didn't like those who hunted them. It was an entirely different thing, however, to hear someone implying they would kill a hunter. I couldn't imagine any of my friends at the Sanctuary saying something like that, and I had to wonder what would happen if someone like Gunnar was face-to-face with a hunter.

It wouldn't go well for the hunter, I was sure, but would Gunnar kill someone? Would Mori, or Zach, or even the witches? That wasn't a rabbit hole I wanted to go down, and before my brain spiraled out of control wondering if my friends were all potential killers, I said, "Thanks for the look, Orin. Any luck on learning more about Baxter's disappearance?"

"Not yet. Everyone in this town seems to have known Baxter, but few know anything about him other than the fact that he ran the Sanctuary and was, by all accounts, a nice guy. His secretiveness kept him safe for decades, but it's also making it harder to find out what happened to him."

"That's not a surprise." Even still, it was disappointing news. "Well, good luck." With that, I moved past Orin and forced myself not to glance over my shoulder to make sure he wasn't following me.

Once I was in the entryway, I decided to stop into Damien's office before I left. As I walked down the hallway that led to it, I realized I had no reason to see him. I wasn't going there to discuss something in particular, and since I had seen him before work that night, there was no need to check in and make sure he was doing okay. We weren't planning to practice our skills that night, either.

So, why am I going, then?

"You need someone to make you feel better."

I jumped at the voice, and I turned to see Zach coming out of his office. He was staring at me with his dark-brown eyes, and I squirmed a little under their intensity. Every now and then, Zach did something in his human form that made it impossible to forget he was a hulking predator three nights a month.

I touched a finger to my temple. "Are you reading my mind, or was I talking to myself?"

"Uh, neither. I'm a werewolf, not a psychic. You have a look like the bogeyman just popped up in front of you. Do you want to talk about it?"

I hitched up one shoulder in a halfhearted shrug, then glanced in the direction I had come from to make sure Orin wasn't lurking anywhere nearby. "The bogeyman *did* just pop up in front of me," I said under my breath. "I was talking to Orin. That knife he got at the antique store is a hunter's weapon. There's a circle carved on it, and he said it's a full moon."

Zach gazed at me placidly. "I know. He showed me."

"Aren't you scared?"

"No. I don't like the guy, but I don't think he's going to kill his client's accountant."

I had to appreciate Zach's courage, as well as his reference to being the Sanctuary's accountant. A werewolf who was good with numbers seemed like such a contradiction.

Zach reached out and took one of my hands. He looked at me intently again, but this time, his gaze was less searching and more reassuring. "Don't let him get under your skin. There's one of him, and a lot of us. He's not going to hurt you, or me, or anyone else here. In fact, I'm on my way upstairs for my shift watching Seraphina. Laura is coming over to sit with me, so there will be two werewolves keeping an eye on our siren."

I felt my nerves calming, and after a deep breath, I was even able to tease Zach a little. "Oh, your girlfriend is coming over?"

Instead of making a snarky comeback, Zach smiled softly. "Yeah."

I blinked. "Oh, wait. You two are actually a couple now?"

"We are. Thanks again for introducing me to her." Zach gave my hand a squeeze then walked away, looking the happiest I had ever seen him.

"Aww," I said quietly to myself. I was happy for Zach and Laura. They were both good people, and I was glad they had found each other.

I hesitated for a moment as I stood there in the hallway. Zach hadn't been reading my mind, but he had been right that I had needed someone to make me feel better. And, after that talk, I did feel better. Maybe I had been heading to Damien's office because my subconscious knew I needed a little pick-me-up.

So why, then, did I still want to see Damien? Almost before I had even made a decision, my feet were carrying me in the direction of his office again.

I was hesitant about going to see Damien when I didn't have a reason to do so, because of the teasing he and I had been enduring the last couple of months. I had teased Zach about having a girlfriend because he had been teasing me about having a boyfriend so often. In fact, "It's not like that!" had become a routine response to people like Clara, Justine, and even Mama whenever they hinted there was something romantic going on between Damien and me.

This time, Damien's office door was open, and when I walked in, he was just putting his black suit coat on. His back arched as he slid his arms into the sleeves, his chest muscles looking especially impressive underneath his well-tailored gray button-down shirt.

I stopped short, staring at him. A little rush ran through me, making me feel slightly lightheaded.

Oh, no, I realized. *It is like that.*

CHAPTER FOURTEEN

"Oh, hi," Damien said as he pulled the jacket into place and buttoned the front. "I figured you had gone home a while ago."

"Nope." My voice was barely above a whisper. *If I don't call attention to myself, maybe he won't know what I'm thinking.* Damien couldn't read minds, but I knew without a shred of doubt my feelings were written all over my face. There was no way I was successfully hiding the shock I felt at my realization.

After months of saying I had absolutely zero interest in a romantic relationship with anyone, and especially not with Damien, I realized I had been completely wrong.

No, I told myself, *I wasn't ready when I first came to Nightmare. But I'm ready now.*

At forty-two years old, what was I even supposed to call this? Saying I had a crush on Damien seemed too high school.

I liked him.

I was interested in him.

I want to put my hands on his shirt and feel those muscles underneath.

I inhaled sharply, and my hand flew to my mouth, as if I had said the words out loud. I knew I had only thought them, but I was so surprised by myself that I felt flustered.

"Olivia? Has something happened? Are you okay?" Damien moved around his desk and came toward me.

So much for not calling attention to myself.

I lowered my hand and stared down at the rug. "I'm fine," I managed. "It's been a night of…surprises."

Damien stopped right in front of me. "What kind of surprises?"

I cleared my throat to buy myself a few seconds. There was no way I was going to confess my feelings to Damien, and talking about a subject as far away from romance as possible seemed like the best course of action. "Did you know that knife Orin got at the antique store is a hunter's weapon?" I asked.

Damien's expression turned dark as I dared to glance up at him. "No. I caught his comment about it having enough silver to kill a werewolf, but I didn't realize it had been specifically made to kill them."

"Is that normal? For a hunter's knife to show up in a store in the middle of nowhere?"

"Supernatural creatures have been living in Nightmare for well over a century. You've met some hunters already, and I'm sure they weren't the first to come here. We can ask Malcolm what he knows, since he's been in Nightmare for so long, but I'm not sure it matters. Orin found a knife, recognized what it was and what kind of value it holds, and he bought it. Where it came from probably isn't relevant."

"Probably not," I agreed.

"What other surprises have you had tonight?" Damien asked the question so innocently.

"Oh, um." I hesitated. "The antique store is reopening tomorrow."

"Already? Seems like they would still be cleaning up the mess the murderer left."

"I thought the same thing." I told Damien about the

flyers and what the two women had said to me, and he wrinkled his nose.

"Tacky," he said when I finished. Then, his shoulders shook in a silent laugh. "And I'm guessing you'll be right there in the middle of it."

"I'm picking up Clara and Justine at noon tomorrow."

"Of course you are." Damien smiled at me. "Let me know if you learn anything."

"I will. Have a good night."

"I'll walk you out. Do you want a ride home?"

Again, I felt flustered. "I drove since it's so cold, but thank you."

He's just asking to be polite, I told myself firmly. *Don't read into it.*

Damien saw me to my car, and soon, I was driving along the one-lane road in the direction of the gallows. "Quit it, Liv," I said to myself. "Calm down and stop being ridiculous. You are not falling for anyone, especially Damien."

But when I got home and crawled into bed, all I could think about was how often Damien and I had been holding hands lately as I tried to help him control his supernatural ability. And I thought back to the night in October, when he had stood so close to me but never got to say whatever he wanted to tell me because we had been interrupted. The look on his face that night, and the way he had said my name...

I buried my head under my pillow. Thoughts of romance made it even more difficult to sleep than thoughts of murder, and I lay awake for a long, long time.

When my alarm went off on Saturday morning, I already knew my brain was going to require some extra cups of coffee.

I was positively jittery by the time I got in my car to drive to the Sanctuary shortly before noon. When I crested the hill and got my first glimpse of the building, I realized I wasn't looking at it but at the cars in the staff parking area to the left of the Sanctuary.

I was looking for Damien's car.

It wasn't there, anyway, and by the time I had parked and walked to the front door, my thoughts had managed to move on to what the scene at the antique store might be like that day. I figured there would be a huge crowd, but beyond that, I had no idea what to expect.

The doors were locked up tight, so I knocked as loudly as I could. About half a minute later, Malcolm opened the door. "Hello, Olivia. Good timing. I was just coming down the stairs in search of breakfast. Would you like pancakes?"

"That's so sweet of you," I said as Malcolm stepped back to let me in. "But I already had breakfast, and I'm ready for a little antique shopping."

"Shopping or sleuthing?" Malcolm asked.

"Maybe a bit of both."

"Okay, but we're going to have to stop for coffee on the way," I heard Justine say. I looked over to see her just coming down the stairs. "I overslept, and I haven't had any yet."

"I've had so much that I'm vibrating," I said, "but we can swing past the coffee shop on our way."

Malcolm set off to make pancakes while Justine and I waited for Clara to join us. Even though Clara's family was in town, she preferred living at the Sanctuary instead of with them. Clara seemed really close to her parents and her sister, and I suspected that not living together under one roof helped maintain the harmonious family relationship.

We heard footsteps echoing from the hallway that led to the dining room, and Justine called, "Come on, already!"

Instead of Clara, though, it was Malcolm who

appeared. He was carrying two steaming mugs of coffee. "Clara is just wrapping up her own breakfast, so I thought I'd bring you two some coffee while you wait."

Justine almost sent the coffee flying as she gave Malcolm a grateful hug, but he managed to keep both mugs upright. As he handed mine to me, he winked. "Yours is decaf."

"Thanks."

We had just finished our coffee when Clara came rushing out of the hallway. "Sorry! I woke up starving, and I figured there was no way I could handle the crowds of shoppers without having some food first."

"You could have had a handful of honey candy," Justine said with a wicked look.

Clara made a face of mock distress. "Oh, you horrible woman! You're trying to kill me with one of my favorite sweets!"

"Since fairies love sugar," I began, glossing over the fact that Justine had just made a joke about the murder of a fairy named Annabelle, "do you eat your pancakes with a whole gallon of maple syrup?"

"Worse," Clara said with a grimace. "I eat kids' cereal."

I snickered. "Great. We'll let you run off all the energy at the antique store."

We turned to head out as Justine said, "Olivia, you'd better start conjuring. I don't want this to be a wasted trip. We're either coming home with clues or something cute!"

"On it," I promised.

And I was. During the drive, I barely listened to the chatter from Clara and Justine because I was focused on conjuring some good results from this trip to the antique store. Considering we had discovered the body of Mrs. Knowles the last time we tried to go, I figured this time around had to be better.

We hadn't even reached the parking lot before we realized just how popular the antique store was. Cars were parked along the shoulder of the road, and people—mostly women my age or a little older—were walking cautiously along the edge of the road, their heads swiveling to keep an eye out for cars.

I kept driving, hoping maybe there would be an open spot in the store's parking lot, but it seemed about a dozen other people had the same idea, and there was a line of cars backed up onto the road, all trying to get into the lot. I waited patiently behind them as they slowly pulled into the parking lot, and then I kept driving straight ahead. As soon as I got past the store, I saw a spot on the side of the road that I could just fit my car into.

"This is going to be interesting," Justine predicted as we climbed out of the car.

"It's going to be claustrophobic," Clara countered.

It was chaos. There was a steady stream of people going both into and out of the front door, and once we had squeezed our way inside, I could see a line about ten people deep at the counter to my left. An employee—with bright-green hair pulled up into a messy bun, I noticed—was stabbing her index finger against the screen of a digital cash register while reaching out with her free hand to take money from a shopper.

Clara was in the lead, and she dodged right, past a clump of old women talking loudly about what a ceramic gravy boat might be worth, and threaded her way into a less-congested area of the store.

It also happened to be right where we had seen Mrs. Knowles's body.

Justine put her hands on Clara's back and nudged her gently forward. "Keep going, please!"

Soon, we were in the aisle farthest from the crowd up

front. There were only a few people browsing nearby, and I paused to enjoy the relative silence.

Justine reached out and lifted a small music box inlaid with turquoise. "Ooh, this would look great in the cabin vignette. We could hide a speaker near it to play a spooky little tune."

"How much is it?" Clara asked. "I know the Sanctuary is on a budget, but remember, all prices have been axed!"

I groaned, but the sound of a man's voice rose over the noise I was making.

"You don't expect me to stop, do you?" the man said.

The three of us all leaned toward the shelf of antiques between us and the next row, looking for a break between items that would let us spy on whomever was speaking. Two people were on the other side of the shelf, a man and a woman. Both of them looked like they were somewhere in their sixties.

"Oh, give it up, Preston," the woman said bitingly.

"No, I won't," the man countered. "This place never rightfully belonged to Mrs. Knowles, and it doesn't belong to you, either! This building is mine!"

CHAPTER FIFTEEN

I heard a murmur, and I peered between a teapot and an antique iron to see several people gathering at the end of the aisle where the argument was taking place. I figured the woman must be Tina, the new owner of the store, but I didn't know who the man might be. However, I vaguely remembered Tanner saying something about someone who had contested Mrs. Knowles's ownership of the store for years, and I wondered if this confrontation was about that.

People were gathering on the other end of the aisle, too, hemming in the man and the woman. Someone in the crowd shouted, "Don't you listen to him, Tina!"

A man standing not far from my vantage point yelled, "Preston's right!"

"This is going to turn into a mob, fast," Justine whispered to Clara and me. "Clara, you and I are going to get this guy Preston under control and away from the crowd. Olivia, you escort Tina outside."

Before I could ask how I was supposed to accomplish that in such a big crowd, Justine and Clara sprang into action. Clearly, this was something they had done before, and I made a mental note to ask them what had transpired at the Sanctuary in the past to make them this confident about their crowd-control skills.

Justine and Clara walked quickly into the aisle where the argument was happening. "Show's over!" Justine called in a loud voice. "Ladies and gentlemen, please return to your shopping. Excuse me, coming through!"

I followed, my jaw probably halfway to the floor, as I watched the crowd obey. They parted to let the three of us through, and people were already turning away and wandering off.

A few folks were still standing there, not budging, but when the two antique chandeliers hanging overhead began to swing wildly, they hustled out of the row pretty quickly. I knew Justine had used her telekinesis to move the chandeliers, rightfully assuming people would choose their safety over sticking around to watch some drama.

I couldn't hear what Justine said to Preston, but soon, she and Clara were flanking him as they headed toward the back of the store. He seemed to be pleading with them, and Clara was looking at him sympathetically.

"Ma'am?" I addressed Tina hesitantly. The woman had a look on her face that made me slightly afraid to talk to her.

"Tina. Tina Dunning. The rightful owner of this place. And don't you dare say otherwise." Tina's hazel eyes flashed behind her wire-rimmed glasses, and I raised my hands instinctively.

"I know you're the rightful owner," I assured her. "But clearly, a few people here disagree with that. Let's head out front and get a little fresh air. We want everyone here to spend money, not stand around watching an argument."

Tina hesitated, then nodded. "Probably a good idea. I might yell at someone, the way I'm feeling."

You already did, I thought as Tina followed me outside. A few people stared as we passed, but no one spoke or tried to stop us.

Once we were outside, I led Tina a short distance away from the door. "Who is that guy, anyway?" I asked.

"Preston Watts, Junior. His daddy owned this building, and he believes it should have gone to him when old Senior died about a million years ago. Preston hounded my sister about this place for decades. Now it's my turn, I suppose."

I frowned. "Was there something illegal about the sale that made Preston feel it's rightfully his?"

"Nope. He got the money from the sale, but he's been raising a fuss for the past forty years, anyway. He says the place is special, and it never should have been sold out from under his family."

I glanced at the old adobe building. It didn't look very special to me, but I figured Preston must have some childhood memories about the place. "We can call the police if he won't leave," I said. "You don't need him down here causing trouble, especially when the place is so busy."

Tina shook her head. "No. They're not real happy with me right now. I had a little, uh, disagreement with Fred while the police were here on Thursday. They had to step in."

"Fred? That's your brother-in-law, right?"

"What Cynthia saw in him, I'll never know. At least she was smart enough not to leave the store to him."

"Do you think he wouldn't have managed it well?"

Tina snorted in derision. "He wouldn't have managed it at all. Fred always said he would sell this place the minute Cynthia died."

Well, that might be a motive for murder. Tanner and McCrory had said there didn't seem to be any love lost between Fred and Cynthia Knowles. Could he have killed his own wife for the money he would get from selling the antique store?

"Cynthia loved this place," Tina continued, reaching

out to brush her fingers against the window. "So do I. I told her I'd keep it open as long as I was able, so she went to see her lawyer and changed her will."

I was too surprised to answer right away. What Tina was telling me about the lawyer wasn't news—Wally Hart himself had told me about Mrs. Knowles changing the will —but I was startled to hear her talking with real compassion about her sister. As it turned out, there was one person in Nightmare who had loved Cynthia Knowles.

"I'm so sorry for your loss," I said. "I can't imagine what the past few days have been like for you."

Tina sniffed and reached up to push a stray dark-gray hair off her forehead. "It's been a sad, shocking time, but I know my sister made the right choice in leaving this place to me. Just look at all the people here to buy the antiques she worked so hard to curate."

I resisted the urge to say that people hadn't really come out to shop, but to gawk at the crime scene. Even as I thought that, though, I saw a woman walk out the door with a large paper bag in her hand. Whatever had brought so many people to the antique store that day, there was no denying they were making purchases.

"I'm Olivia, by the way," I said, realizing I hadn't introduced myself.

"Olivia, I appreciate you and your friends standing up for me. Now that things have settled down, I'm going to head inside to make sure everything is going smoothly." Tina gave me a nod, then went back inside.

I stood where I was for a few moments, simply enjoying the peace and quiet. Diving back into the crowded store wasn't something I was looking forward to, but I needed to find Justine and Clara. I had taken my first step when I spotted Preston Watts coming around the side of the building. He must have left through the back door.

I waved at Preston, and he hesitated for a moment

before walking up to me. He was a tall man, and I was sure he had been well-built in his younger years. He still moved with the easy fluidity of someone who was fit. When he reached me, Preston stopped a few feet away. "If you're going to lecture me, I don't need it."

"Lecture you? No, I was just going to ask if you're okay. That was a tense moment inside the store."

Preston's shoulders relaxed, and he looked slightly abashed. "I didn't mean to make a scene like that. I never should have yelled at Tina, but she's as stubborn as her sister was."

"She mentioned your father used to own this building. Was he an antique dealer, too?"

"No, this was his print shop. Some of the old equipment is still in the back room. This place is special to me."

Special enough to kill for? I wondered. Preston would have known that murdering Cynthia Knowles wouldn't get him the building, but if he knew her husband was going to sell the place after her death, he might have hurried things along a little bit with an axe. Preston could have bought the building from Cynthia's husband, and he'd be happy knowing it was back in his family.

"I was surprised to hear Tina is inheriting the store, rather than Fred Knowles," I said as casually as if I were talking about the weather.

"It is a surprise," Preston agreed. "Especially since the two of them have barely spoken for the past ten years. I've never seen two siblings hate each other so much."

CHAPTER SIXTEEN

"That can't be right," I blurted. "Tina just stood here and got a little misty-eyed about how much her sister loved this store."

"Then she's a great actress," Preston said, snorting out a laugh. "How she wound up being the beneficiary is beyond me. The two of them had a falling out years ago over some joint real estate venture that ended badly. Mrs. Knowles must have changed the will before that happened."

I shook my head. "No, the change was made just a few months ago. Her lawyer said it was toward the end of last year."

Preston raised an eyebrow, his forehead wrinkling. "Only a few months ago, huh? And now, Tina is lamenting the loss of her sister, like they actually loved each other. Hmm."

There was no need for Preston to say what he was thinking. Tina suddenly looked very suspicious. If what Preston was saying were true—I had to remind myself he might be trying to shift suspicion away from himself—then why in the world had Mrs. Knowles changed her will? Why do something nice for her sister after a decade of holding a grudge?

"Mrs. Knowles didn't deserve what she got," Preston

said suddenly. "I'm not going to miss her one bit, but I am sorry she went out in such a violent way."

"Why does everyone call her Mrs. Knowles rather than Cynthia?" I asked suddenly. Since Mrs. Knowles was older, I had assumed it was done out of respect, but Tina was probably only a couple of years younger than her sister, and Preston was calling Tina by her first name.

Preston chuckled darkly. "You didn't know her well, did you?"

"I didn't know her at all," I admitted. "I haven't been in Nightmare for long."

"She insisted on being called Mrs. Knowles. From what I understand, she began demanding it on the day of her wedding, and anyone foolish enough to call her Cynthia would get an earful. I think getting married was a milestone for her, a show of just how perfect her life had become. Her parents had been poor, and she was proud of the fact that she had built herself a nice, middle-class life. She even put a white picket fence around her house."

I nodded. I had known plenty of people like that in my lifetime. "She wanted all the appearance of a good life, even if she was miserable for every second of it."

"Precisely." Preston turned at the sound of screeching car tires, and I followed his gaze to see a blue sedan stopped right in front of the store.

A man about the same age as Preston and Tina climbed out of the driver's side, and I heard Preston mutter, "Oh, no."

"Oh, no, what?" I asked him quietly.

"It's Fred Knowles."

The man headed straight for us. He didn't move as quickly and easily as Preston, and Preston could easily have slipped away, but he stayed right where he was, staring defiantly at Fred.

Fred's salt-and-pepper hair was thinning, and his

tortoise-shell glasses were slightly askew. He stabbed a finger in Preston's direction. "Get off my wife's property!"

Preston folded his arms over his chest. "It's not your wife's property anymore, Fred. Besides, I was trying to leave, but this lady stopped me."

Fred's dark eyes turned to me, and I wanted to duck behind Preston to get out of his line of sight. He was furious.

"And who are you?" Fred roared.

"I just came here to shop." I took a step backward. I didn't want to mention the argument between Tina and Preston. Fred would learn about it soon enough, and there was no need to exacerbate an already-tense situation.

"Lovely talking to you," Preston said sarcastically to me. Without another look at Fred or me, he set off toward the far end of the parking lot.

That left me alone with Fred, which wasn't the ideal situation. *Fred will calm down and be helpful,* I repeated in my mind. It was what I wanted most at that moment, and I knew I could conjure it if I just focused enough.

That was hard to do, since Fred was still staring me down. With Preston gone, his ire seemed to have shifted to me.

Fred will calm down and be helpful.

Suddenly, Fred's face crumpled, and he covered his eyes with one hand. He gave a loud sniff.

"Mr. Knowles?" *Oh, dear, this isn't what I had in mind.*

"I'm a mess," he said in a thick voice. He dropped his hand and looked at me, all the anger in his eyes replaced with sorrow. "It was bad enough Cynthia got killed. Then, to know she didn't even love me enough to give me the store…"

I looked at Fred sympathetically. He might have been mean and scary, but he was also grieving. "I'm sure the money from selling this place would have been helpful."

"I had to look at the will myself before I would believe it. I still don't believe it."

"I understand your wife and her sister didn't get along that well. Why would Mrs. Knowles leave the antique store to someone she didn't like?"

Fred shrugged, his eyes moving toward the front door. "Tina showed up here one day last fall. Cynthia told me. She started talking about patching things up and making amends, all that. Cynthia told her it was going to take more than shallow apologies. We lost a lot of money investing in a real estate venture that Tina talked us into, you know."

"So I've heard. That explains the bad blood between them."

"Tina refused to give up. She kept hounding Cynthia, saying they were sisters, and it wasn't right for there to be so much animosity between them. Cynthia finally gave in."

I tilted my head. "It's one thing to forgive a sister. It's another thing to change your will to give her the one thing that has value."

Fred spread his hands and sighed. "I have no idea how Tina talked her into that. We lost money in that real estate venture, and it was all Tina's fault. Now, I'm losing money because of her again. Cynthia should have let me keep the store."

"So you could sell it and get some of that lost money back?"

"Exactly. I know Cynthia loved this place, but no one— not even Tina—is going to pour the effort into maintaining it the way she did. It's going to be a shadow of what it once was. Why keep it going when it could help me financially? It's not like Cynthia would even know if it had been sold. She'd be dead! She *is* dead, and she has no idea what kind of stress she's creating for everyone, all because of this stupid store full of old junk!"

Fred had been getting wound up again, his voice rising and his hands curling into fists. He cut off abruptly when a shrill scream sounded from inside.

My first thought was that someone had found another dead body. My second thought was that Justine and Clara were probably still inside. I turned and raced toward the door, Fred following as quickly as he could.

When I got inside, I saw Tina standing in front of a display of old clocks. At her feet was a broken wooden clock, its gears scattered across the floor. Tina was staring down a woman with a baby on her hip. "You break it, you buy it!" Tina screeched.

"I didn't touch it!" the woman countered. When her baby made a noise that promised tears weren't far off, she lowered her voice, but her tone was just as firm. "The clock fell off the shelf."

"It didn't fall," said a man standing just in front of me. He seemed to be talking to himself, and neither Tina nor the woman with the baby heard him. "It launched into the air."

My eyes darted toward the display of clocks, then up into the rafters above us. Fred had just said Cynthia wouldn't even know about all the stress she was causing, because she was dead.

Except, maybe, Cynthia knew exactly what was going on. Just because she was dead, didn't mean she was gone.

CHAPTER SEVENTEEN

Tina and the woman were still staring each other down. *Seriously, can't this lady go half an hour without getting into a confrontation with someone?* The baby gurgled, then began to cry.

"You have to pay for it. No one else was near the clock," Tina said, oblivious to the baby.

Fred pushed past me. "Tina, enough! The lady says she didn't touch it."

Tina rounded on Fred. "You can't tell me how to run my business! You have no right to be here, anyway."

"I have every right. This was my wife's store!"

A few bystanders watched eagerly, but most people began slowly backing away. Several people who had items in their hands plunked them down onto shelves and marched out of the store, probably disgusted by Tina's entire demeanor. First, she had been yelling at a woman with a crying baby, and now, she was yelling at a man whose wife had been murdered only two days before.

Not exactly a good start to her time as the owner of Mining Town Antiques.

I spotted Clara's silvery hair nearby, and I headed in that direction. As soon as I reached my friends, Justine took my arm and steered me toward the back of the store, where only a few shoppers were browsing.

"I saw the clock fall," Clara said quietly. "It flew off the shelf like someone had pushed it."

"Which means," I said excitedly, "Mrs. Knowles might still be here, after all."

"Exactly!" Clara nudged Justine. "Unless someone moved it with their mind."

"It wasn't me. I think Mrs. Knowles is still here, and she isn't happy with the new management."

"She and her sister only recently patched things up," I said. Quickly, I filled them in on my conversations with Tina, Preston, and Fred.

When I was finished, Clara began to giggle. "You've been busy! You've talked to three suspects in the time it took me to pick out a piece of costume jewelry!" She lifted a hand, a necklace made from faux diamonds and sapphires dangling from her fingers.

"It's pretty, but where in Nightmare is fancy enough for a necklace like that?" I asked.

"Anywhere is fancy enough if I decide it is," Clara said. "I have a little black dress this will look divine with. Now, I just need a hot boyfriend to take me somewhere I can wear it."

Justine nodded her head toward me. "Ask Olivia. She knows where to find the hot boyfriends."

I opened my mouth to give my usual response, but instead, I waggled my eyebrows at Clara. "Maybe Damien has a secret brother," I told her.

All three of us laughed, but we cut off abruptly at the sound of something hitting the concrete floor near us. We all looked around wildly, and Justine gasped. "There! The cast-iron pan!" She pointed at a pan that was upside-down in the middle of the aisle.

"Sorry, Mrs. Knowles!" Clara called, gazing at the space above our heads. "We're not laughing at you. In fact, we're trying to help you!"

"We need to bring Tanner and McCrory here to have a little chat with Mrs. Knowles," I said. "I'll just have to make them promise to be nice to her."

"That's a great idea," Justine agreed. "But first, we shop!"

We spent the next half hour browsing up and down the aisles, turning and heading in the opposite direction anytime we spotted Tina roving around angrily. I found a pretty trinket box that had *Nightmare* carved into the lid. It looked like a souvenir from decades before, when tourists had made Nightmare a popular road-trip stop in the nineteen fifties and sixties.

"I'm buying this," I said, waving it toward Clara and Justine. "Let's hope this antique box doesn't come with ghosts attached!"

"Unless there are tiny six-shooters in there, I don't think you have to worry about it," Justine assured me.

Justine had two baskets and an old spittoon in her arms. "I think our work here is done. These are going to look great inside the haunt."

We made our way to the front of the store, where the counter with the cash register sat. The crowd had thinned significantly, so there were only two people ahead of us in line. I didn't spot Tina anywhere nearby, and I let out a breath I hadn't realized I'd been holding.

When I stepped up to the register to pay, I finally had a chance to chat with Wanda, the longtime employee with the green hair. Wanda looked like she was in her mid- to late-twenties, and her expression was equal parts bored and exhausted.

Wanda was wearing a black blouse, and a large silver pentagram hung from a chain around her neck.

"Oh," I said, hooking a thumb under my own necklace. "We have similar jewelry."

Wanda eyed me skeptically. "You're a witch, too?"

"No, though I do know a few witches."

"So why the pentagram, then?"

"The necklace was a gift."

"From her boyfriend," Clara added.

"It's got protection spells on it," I said, completely ignoring Clara. I hoped dropping that information might give me a bit of an in with Wanda.

Wanda's face lit up. "Cool," she said, looking at my necklace with new appreciation. She tapped at the screen in front of her. "Fourteen dollars and thirty-two cents. I gave you a discount since we're kindred spirits."

We were not kindred spirits, because I would never throw a party to celebrate someone's murder, but I smiled in real appreciation. I still kept myself to a budget, albeit not as strict of one as I'd had when I first arrived in Nightmare, and I was grateful whenever I got to save a bit of money.

I handed over a twenty-dollar bill. "Are there often yelling matches here?"

"I've seen more than I can count. Cynthia and customers she dislikes, Cynthia and Tina, Cynthia and Preston, Cynthia and Fred. Tina taking on customers is a new one, though."

I noted that Wanda called Mrs. Knowles by her first name. An act of defiance, I supposed.

"How can you stand working here with so much negativity?" I asked.

Wanda touched the pentagram she wore. "Lots of spell work. For positivity, so the bad vibes won't stick to me, so people will just get along, that sort of thing. I do some free-lance spell work, if you ever need help with anything."

"I'll keep that in mind," I said politely. "Do you feel like your spells make a difference?"

Wanda looked thoughtful. "They do help me. I feel like

there's an invisible wall between me and all the anger, so all that bad energy can't stick to me. When I leave here in the evenings, I leave all the bad stuff behind."

That sounded nice. I would have to ask Morgan, Madge, and Maida if they could cook up anything like that for me. It would be handy if I ever wanted to go antique shopping again and might run into Tina. Plus, it could be helpful at crime scenes.

"Maybe things will settle down soon," I said hopefully.

"Tina will always find something to be mad about," Wanda said with a shake of her head as she handed my change to me. "I only worked three days a week with Cynthia. She was off my other two days. And, when she was in, I was usually in the back, taking care of online sales. That helped me stay away from the worst of the drama. Oh, here, take a card for the online store. There's some good stuff on there."

I took the card and the small bag with my vintage Nightmare box in it. "Good luck," I told Wanda.

"I don't need luck," Wanda said with a smile. "I have magic."

Justine and Clara paused to admire a broach in the jewelry case next to the register as we were on our way out. "I thought we were done shopping?" I joked as I sailed past them.

I pulled open the front door and strode out, only to run right into Officer Reyes.

"Oh, no," he said with a groan.

"Hello to you, too," I said. I held up my bag. "I swear, we were just shopping! I found a cute little souvenir box."

I moved to one side so Clara and Justine could get through the door, too. Justine lifted her chin and looked at Reyes over her armful of items. "Hi, Officer Reyes. We have to stop meeting like this."

"I was just thinking the same thing. Can I help you with that, Ms. Abbott?" Without waiting for an answer, Reyes reached out and lifted the spittoon out of Justine's arms.

"Thank you," she said. "That's much better."

Reyes tucked the spittoon under one arm while he held up his notebook with his free hand. "Since you three have been shopping, maybe you saw something helpful. Did you spot any items with symbols like this on them?"

Reyes turned his notebook toward us, and I saw a line of symbols drawn down the center of the page. There was a circle, a wonky-looking triangle, a lazy *S*, and something that looked like elongated quotation marks.

All three of us shook our heads, and I felt Clara's fingers against my arm. "I think," she said pointedly, "Olivia mentioned seeing some of these symbols somewhere."

Clara wanted me to tell Reyes about Orin's knife. Before, when we had discovered Mrs. Knowles sprawled on the floor of the antique store, Clara and Justine had both advised me against naming Orin as a suspect. After all, we didn't know of any motive he might have had for killing Mrs. Knowles. Now, though, maybe for her own peace of mind, Clara wanted me to tell Reyes what I knew.

Justine looked at me and gave just the slightest nod.

"I've seen those first two symbols," I told Reyes. I felt my chest tighten. If I got Orin into trouble, I didn't want to know how he might react. My hand strayed to my necklace, and I thought of the protection spells on it. I took a deep breath. "There's a man staying at the Sanctuary right now. He's doing a little consulting work for the haunt. He bought a knife here that has that same circle and triangle on it."

Reyes put the spittoon down and pulled out a pen. He

flipped to a fresh page in his notebook and began to write. "Interesting. He got it here, you say?"

"Yes," I confirmed. "Why do the symbols matter, though? What do they have to do with the murder?"

Reyes paused in his writing and looked up. "Those symbols I showed you are inscribed on the axe that was used to kill Cynthia Knowles."

CHAPTER EIGHTEEN

It wasn't just a random hunter's knife that had shown up at the antique store. There had been a hunter's axe, too. Had an entire stash of hunter's weapons wound up at Mining Town Antiques?

Again, I thought of Jeff Crosley. Maybe he had downsized when he gave up the hunter's life and opened The Lusty Lunch Counter. I was going to have to talk to him to find out if one of his old weapons had been used to kill Mrs. Knowles.

"What's the name of this consultant?" Reyes asked.

"Orin," I said. I looked at Justine. "I don't know his last name."

"Pierce," Justine supplied. "I think. I'm not working with him much."

"This is helpful information," Reyes said. He looked at me pointedly. "I'm surprised you didn't mention the knife when we chatted before."

"None of us thought it was relevant," Clara said with a shrug, "especially since we didn't know about the symbols on both weapons. We discussed Orin and his knife after we got done giving you our statements, but why would someone from out of town want to kill Mrs. Knowles? There was no reason for us to think Orin was a suspect."

I wanted to hug Clara for standing up for me. "And

then," I added, "when we found out Mrs. Knowles had been killed with an axe, the information seemed even more irrelevant."

"Too much information is better than too little," Reyes pointed out. "Next time there's a murder, and you know someone has recently purchased a weapon from the victim, you might want to let me know."

"Noted," I said. I was surprised to feel a twinge of remorse. I felt like I had let Reyes down, and I was possibly more disappointed than he was.

I also felt like I had just created a world of trouble for Orin, and even though my first thoughts had been about my own safety, I suddenly worried the situation might impede the search for Baxter. "Officer Reyes? Er, Luis? If you do talk to Orin, can you please leave my name out of the discussion?"

"Of course." Reyes picked up the spittoon again. "I'll carry this to your car. Where are you parked?"

We trooped to my parking spot on the side of the road. I brought up the rear, and even though I was watching Justine and Reyes chat, my mind was on Orin and how he would react if the police came looking for him.

Once we had loaded our purchases into my trunk and said goodbye to Reyes, we climbed into the car and sat for a moment.

"Well," I said.

"Well," Clara and Justine agreed in unison.

"What a wild day," Justine said, leaning her head back against the headrest and closing her eyes.

"You know what we need after all this excitement?" I said. "A cheeseburger and fries."

"I'll be having waffles, thank you very much," Clara announced. When I craned my neck around to look at her in the back seat, she shrugged. "What? You mentioned syrup this morning, and now I'm craving it. The Lusty serves breakfast all day."

Justine opened her eyes. "Do you want a cheeseburger, Olivia, or do you want to talk to that guy who owns the place? The former hunter."

"Both," I admitted. "Jeff might be the one who sold the knife and the axe to the antique store. Knowing where they came from won't help us find the killer, but I want to talk to him out of curiosity."

"A cheeseburger sounds amazing," Justine said, her eyes fluttering closed again. "Wake me when we get there."

The Lusty Lunch Counter got its name from the fact it was in a ramshackle building from the eighteen hundreds that had once housed a brothel. It looked Wild West on the outside, but the inside looked like a diner from the nineteen fifties. The building wasn't far from High Noon Boulevard, the street where tourists flocked to see the old buildings decked out to look like they had back in Nightmare's mining boom days. The street the diner was on was mostly devoid of tourists, which made The Lusty a nice place for locals.

Before long, we were seated at a booth, cushioned by the overstuffed red leather benches. Justine really had fallen asleep during the short drive, and she looked around groggily as we waited for our server. She perked up a bit after gulping down half a soda.

Once we had eaten our late lunch, it was time to talk to Jeff. Justine and Clara declined the offer to visit his office with me. They were both nursing cups of coffee—Clara took hers with a shocking amount of sugar—and they were content to stay put. Plus, as Justine rightly pointed out, Jeff might be more comfortable talking about his hunter past without being stared down by three supernatural creatures.

Three. It was strange counting myself as a supernatural creature. I was still getting used to the fact that I was a conjuror, but I could no longer deny that I really did have a supernatural ability.

I walked to the stainless steel counter and hopped up onto an empty stool. Since it was well after the lunch rush, only a few of them were occupied. My friend Ella was behind the counter. She had come over to say hello while we ate, and she bustled over to me with a little smile.

"See that table over your right shoulder?" she asked. Her big hoop earrings swung as she looked in that direction.

I glanced back. "The four women? Yeah. Why?"

"They were at the antique store today, and they said you and your friends did a great job keeping a fight from breaking out." Ella twirled the end of her long dark ponytail with one hand. "You can't even go shopping without finding trouble."

"It does seem to be one of my talents."

"Anyway, they were so impressed that they have decided to buy dessert for all of you. Your server is over at your table now, but go ahead and tell me what you'd like, and I'll make sure it gets over to you."

Wow. Free dessert? Our day had just taken a nice turn. I told Ella I'd love a slice of the apple pie, then added, "I'm actually over here to ask if Jeff is in. I wanted to say hi."

Ella didn't know about Nightmare's supernatural community, so I couldn't tell her why I wanted to talk to Jeff. Luckily, me wanting to see him didn't seem strange, and she waved toward the swinging door that led into the kitchen. "Head on back. He'll be glad to see you."

I slid off the stool and walked behind the counter to the kitchen. Jeff's office was in one corner of it, and it was no bigger than a closet. In fact, I suspected it had been designed for storage rather than a desk and chair.

"Hi, Jeff," I called from the doorway. "Can I have a moment?"

There must have been something in my voice or expression that alerted Jeff, and he stood instantly. "Let's go out back," he suggested. "I could use some fresh air."

I followed Jeff out the back door wordlessly. Once we were outside, he turned to me with a concerned look. "This has something to do with the murder, doesn't it?"

Startled, I said, "How did you know?"

Jeff gave me a lopsided smile. "You and I usually only meet when murder is involved."

Add him to the list alongside Reyes.

"Though," Jeff continued, "I can't imagine how I would be connected."

"Do you know what Mrs. Knowles was killed with?" I asked.

"An axe."

"A hunter's axe."

Jeff's mouth fell open. He began to say something several times but stopped. Finally, he leaned against the side of the building and ran a hand through his thinning hair. "You're sure it was a hunter's axe?"

I described the symbols Reyes had shown us in his notebook, then added that someone staying at the Sanctuary had bought a knife with some of the same symbols on it. "Two hunter's weapons somehow wound up on the shelves at the antique store. I thought maybe they were yours."

Jeff shook his head firmly. "No. No way. I would never release those out into the world. I passed a few of them along to other hunters, and I kept some for myself. I might not be a hunter anymore, but that doesn't mean I shouldn't protect myself against monsters." Before I could protest his choice of words, Jeff added in a rush, "And I don't mean your friends at the Sanctuary. You know as well as I do there are bad ones out there, Olivia."

"I know. The tooth fairy who bought the knife might

be one of them, but we need his help trying to find Baxter."

"There's a tooth fairy in town?" Jeff's eyebrows drew together, and he pursed his lips. After a moment, he shook his head, almost imperceptibly, then said, "I don't like that these weapons wound up in the antique store. Way out here, in Nightmare? There's more to the story."

"Agreed," I said. "As I told Justine and Clara, finding their former owner won't solve the murder, but it will satisfy my curiosity."

Jeff raised an eyebrow. "It could solve the murder. You're making the assumption the axe was an item for sale at the store, but it might have still been in someone's private collection. Find the person who sold the knife to the store, and you might find the owner of the axe—and your killer."

CHAPTER NINETEEN

Gobsmacked was a word I never used, but it was what I felt at Jeff's pronouncement. "We've been assuming the axe was on sale at the antique store, and the killer grabbed it because it was the nearest convenient murder weapon," I told him. "And when I say 'we,' I mean the police, too. I understand Reyes has been thinking along the same lines."

"I'd start by going to the store and asking where the knife came from," Jeff said. "Though you might not want to say why you're asking."

I stared at a cracked piece of wooden siding on the building, its color faded to a dull gray. I wasn't seeing it. Rather, I was picturing striking up another conversation with Wanda. "I'll say I saw the knife and am interested in getting something similar. Something that looks as magical as that one."

"Hunters aren't magical," Jeff pointed out.

I blinked and returned my gaze to him. "I know, but there's a young woman working at the store who says she's a witch. And you have to admit, the scrollwork and the symbols on the weapons do give off a magical look, like they should be used for doing spells."

Jeff grumbled something about hunters turning into the very things they were after.

I smiled at Jeff. "Thank you. You've been really helpful.

Now, if you'll excuse me, I have a free slice of pie to enjoy."

We walked back inside, and less than a minute later, I was sinking my teeth into a gooey bite of apple pie.

Clara and Justine were staring at me, their own desserts forgotten for the moment. "This is not fair," Justine said. "Why do you have to eat your dessert before telling us what Jeff said?"

I swallowed. "Just the first bite!" I waved for them to lean over the table. No one was sitting near us, but I didn't want there to be any chance we might be overheard. "Jeff suggested the hunter's axe might not have been something for sale at the store, but something still in the original owner's collection. In other words, someone could have shown up at the antique store with the axe."

"We know the murder was premeditated because of Fiona's flash on Wednesday night," Clara said. "The idea that the killer arrived with the axe in hand makes more sense."

"And it means that if we can track down the person who sold the knife to the store, we might have found our killer," I finished.

Justine pointed at her untouched slice of pumpkin pie. The whipped cream was beginning to droop. "I'm going to eat every crumb of this, and then we're going to collect Tanner and McCrory for another trip to the antique store. While they chat with Mrs. Knowles, we can chat with that green-haired girl."

"Wanda," I supplied. I raised my fork like I was giving a toast. "To solving a murder!"

On our way out of the diner, we thanked the four women who had bought our dessert. They told us what good, responsible young women we were, and I left the diner feeling like I had four unofficial grandmothers. I hadn't bothered to correct them on the "young" part. Justine and Clara qualified, but I certainly didn't.

When I pulled up in front of the Sanctuary, I again found myself looking for Damien's car. It still wasn't there, which was surprising since the afternoon was wearing on, and he was usually in his office well before I arrived for the family meeting each night.

And Damien's office was exactly where we had to go to retrieve the six-shooter box. Luckily, since Justine was the manager of the Sanctuary, she had a key to every room in the building. Clara and I lingered in the entryway and gave an update to Zach, who had come out of his office at the sound of our arrival. We filled him in while Justine retrieved the worn wooden box.

When Justine rejoined us, I saw Tanner and McCrory gliding along in her wake. They were both hooting with laughter.

"What good luck!" McCrory said, holding his sides.

"We actually get to meet the ghost of Mrs. Knowles!" Tanner threw his hat into the air.

"To help us get information from her," I said, sounding like a scolding parent. "We need you two to be polite, so she'll open up to you."

"Aw, that's no fun," Tanner said. I knew he was frowning underneath his red bandana.

"If you say so." McCrory was usually all about following the rules, but he was clearly disappointed he couldn't razz Mrs. Knowles a bit. *She must have been really awful to them*, I thought.

"Want to tag along?" I asked Zach.

"Thanks, but I think your car is going to be crowded enough as it is." Zach retreated into his office, and the rest of us hit the road for our second trip to the antique store that day.

I had only been driving for about half a minute when

Justine suddenly said, "Let's stop at Cowboy's Corral first. Mama is the gossip queen of Nightmare, right? She might know something about a local with a fancy weapons collection."

McCrory cleared his throat, and I glanced in the rearview mirror in time to see him straighten his collar. "An excellent idea," he said.

I had to smile at McCrory's crush on Mama. Even Theo had once asked her out, back when she was young and single.

Talking to Mama couldn't hurt, and it wouldn't be too long of a detour, so I happily agreed with Justine's suggestion. Soon, we were all trooping into the motel office. Justine had the six-shooter box tucked under her arm. Tanner and McCrory were able to roam all over the Sanctuary, even though the guns they were tethered to resided in Damien's office. I knew my car was parked close enough to the motel office that we could have left the box in the car, but it felt better to keep a close eye on it.

I heard Mama talking in a bright voice when I came through the door, and I saw a couple standing at the counter. I gestured wildly at the ghosts, who dove behind the brochure rack.

Mama finished checking the couple in, and as soon as they left, Tanner and McCrory re-emerged. So much afternoon sunshine was streaming through the windows that their forms could barely be seen, but it didn't stop McCrory from sailing right up to Mama, tipping his hat, and saying, "You're looking just as gorgeous as ever, ma'am."

Mama laughed. "It's good to see you, too. What brings all of you to my motel?"

Before any of us could answer, I heard loud footsteps on the stairs. Lucy came bounding into the room a few seconds later, grinning. "I thought I heard a ghost! Oh, and hi!" Lucy went from me to Clara to Justine, giving all of us a tight hug around the waist. When she was done, she threw an apologetic look at Tanner and McCrory. "Sorry I can't hug you two."

"That's okay, little lady," Tanner said, bending at the waist so he was eye-level with Lucy. "Say, that's a real sparkly shirt you're wearing. Are those real diamonds?"

Lucy grabbed her hot-pink T-shirt by the hem and held it out so she could inspect the swirl of rhinestones on it. "Maybe. I don't know."

"No, Tanner," Mama said with a chuckle, "you cannot rob my granddaughter. Those aren't diamonds, anyway."

"I wasn't going to rob her," Tanner said, sounding slightly offended. "I was merely going to advise Lucy on the best places to sell diamonds." He looked at Lucy again and said in a stage whisper, "Nowhere legal, of course."

"The reason we came, Mama," I said in an effort to get us back on track, "is that we wanted to test your knowledge of Nightmare locals."

"Hey, Lucy," Clara cut in, "isn't there a soda machine somewhere here at the motel? Can you take me to it? I'm so thirsty."

Lucy held out her hand. "Right this way!"

"Thanks," I whispered to Clara as she passed me, her hand in Lucy's. Once they had gone out the front door, I told Mama about the markings on both Orin's knife and the murder weapon. "Jeff Crosley is the only former hunter I know in this town, and he says those things aren't his," I finished.

Mama leaned her elbows against the countertop and gazed toward the front window. Slowly, she began to shake her head. "I can't think of anyone in this town who might have sold them to the antique store. If a local has a collection like that, then they aren't talking about it. At least, not with me or any of the circles I run in."

It had been a long shot to ask Mama about the weapons, so I wasn't surprised she didn't know about a secret hunter's stash. Not willing to give up just yet, though, I asked, "Do you know anything about this Preston Watts guy? He says the building the antique store is in was his dad's, and he feels like it should have stayed in the family instead of being sold to Mrs. Knowles."

"Oh, that old argument," Mama said dismissively. "Everyone knows about Junior's grudge. He's been saying for years and years that building should be his. He'll go to his grave still complaining about it."

"We thought maybe he sent someone to their grave," Justine said.

Mama looked like she wanted to laugh. "I can't imagine Preston killing anyone, let alone Mrs. Knowles! Then again, I guess most murderers don't seem like the type, do they? Otherwise, it would be easy to solve every case."

"Preston is staying on my suspect list," I said. "We saw him and Tina Denning get into it at the store earlier today, and he's definitely got a lot of pent-up resentment. He claims the building has sentimental value."

"It might have more value than that." Mama looked at both Justine and me, then added, "There have been rumors for years about a secret room in the building. People say it's full of occult items, and that's what Preston is really after. He doesn't care about the building at all. He just wants the hidden treasure!"

CHAPTER TWENTY

Mama started to laugh heartily. "Maybe that's where the mysterious knife and axe came from! The secret vault of occult treasures!"

She was making a joke out of it, but I considered the secret room a real possibility. "Maybe there is a room with rare and valuable antiques in it, occult or not," I suggested. "Maybe Mrs. Knowles brings out one or two expensive pieces at a time to sell off."

"That rumor has been around for years," Mama said. "I even asked Preston about it once. He said it's a ridiculous notion, and I got the sense he was telling the truth. If the room does exist, then Preston likely isn't looking for it."

"And you're usually right about people," I said. Too bad. I kind of liked the idea of a hidden treasure room.

"Obviously, when I heard there were occult items at the antique store, I wanted to make sure nothing from the Sanctuary had found its way there," Mama continued. "When Preston said the secret room was an unfounded rumor, I stopped worrying about it."

"If no one has found this room," Justine pointed out, "then why does the rumor still exist?"

"The internet," Mama said without hesitation. "That secret room theory has popped up on websites for alternative tourism."

I tilted my head, confused, but Justine was nodding. "Of course. The Sanctuary winds up on those, too."

"Alternative tourism?" I asked.

"You know, the tourist sights outside the usual historic buildings and theme parks," Justine said. "Alternative tourism caters to people who want to see the old cemeteries, the abandoned buildings, places that are a little more weird than the usual tourist fare..."

"Like a year-round haunted house attraction in a former hospital," I said. That made sense.

"And an antique store with a secret room and ties to the occult," Mama added.

If there were any truth to the rumor—and there probably wasn't—who might know of the room's existence outside of Preston and Mrs. Knowles? Would Mrs. Knowles have told Tina about it? Did Wanda know? If Wanda was a witch, then she might know all about a roomful of occult antiques.

"There are two people standing right here who can tell us about any hidden spaces at the antique store," Justine suddenly said. "Tanner? McCrory? You two are being awfully quiet."

Both ghosts started to snicker. "We were just having fun watching you three talk about it," Tanner confessed. "We know that rumor well, because we always had fun watching people hunt for it. One man even crawled underneath a tall shelf and felt around for a trap door in the wall behind it. He just about got stuck, and when all his squirming around knocked half a dozen items onto the floor, Mrs. Knowles made him pay for every single one."

"We were hoping to watch you ladies go in search of it, to be honest," McCrory added. "But you wouldn't have had any luck. We never saw any evidence that such a room exists."

"Heh. The living are so gullible!" Tanner shifted so one

elbow appeared to be leaning on the countertop, even though his arm would go right through the Formica if he dropped it any lower.

"Lucy's back," Mama said quickly, right before the bell above the door rang. Sure enough, Lucy and Clara were coming in, both with grape sodas in their hands.

"I guess it's time for us to head to the antique store," I said. "Secret room or not, we still need to have a talk with Mrs. Knowles."

"Are you having a séance?" Mama asked, surprised.

At the same time, Clara squealed, "Secret room?"

"The ladies will fill you in on that," Tanner said to Clara. Then, he turned to Mama. "No séance. Her ghost appears to be haunting the place, so me and the sheriff are going to have a little reunion with her."

"A polite reunion," I reminded him.

"Look at me," Tanner said, gesturing down at his barely visible duster. "I'm a perfect gentleman."

We said goodbye to Lucy, then made our way to the antique store. The crowd that had been there earlier in the day had thinned significantly, and there were only about a dozen cars in the parking lot. That was good because it meant there was less chance of the ghosts being spotted by someone. Even still, Justine instructed Tanner and McCrory to use extra caution as they went in search of Mrs. Knowles.

When we walked into the store, Wanda was sitting behind the cash register, looking bored. She gave us a brief glance and mumbled, "Good afternoon." Then, she did a double take, her head snapping up as she recognized us. "You're back."

"We are," I said. It was that moment I realized we needed a reason for our return, because telling Wanda that we'd brought our ghosts to chat with her ghost probably wouldn't go over very well.

Thankfully, Clara came to the rescue. She was carrying the six-shooter box this time, and she lifted it to show Wanda. "I was hoping you could look at this and tell me if it's valuable or not."

I almost laughed, which would have ruined the ruse. The six-shooters inside were valuable antiques all on their own, but their historic value, I knew, would really hike up their resale price.

Wanda wrinkled her nose. "That box has seen better days, though it's definitely old." Since she had only worked at Mining Town Antiques for a few years, she had no idea the box had been purchased from that very store. She also didn't know there was anything inside it.

"So it's not worth much?" Clara asked, sounding disappointed.

"Probably not. Sorry," Wanda said.

"Okay. Well, it was worth asking." Clara turned to Justine and me. "While we're here, I want to go look at that painting again. I really think it might be a good fit for the cabin vignette."

"After you," I said. We followed Clara down an aisle to the back of the store, where a door marked *Employees Only* separated the store from what I assumed was storage and office space in the back.

"Boys," Justine hissed. "Anything?"

We waited a handful of seconds, but there was no response. We had to hope Tanner and McCrory were already deep in conversation with Mrs. Knowles.

Justine's phone rang just then, and she answered with, "Hey, Zach." After a brief pause, she said, "I meant to forewarn you, but he got there faster than I expected."

Justine looked at us. "Reyes," she whispered.

So Officer Reyes had already followed up on the lead I had given him. "It's my fault he's there," I said.

"It is not your fault," Justine said. "No, Zach, I wasn't

talking to you, I was telling—okay, fine. Here." She handed her phone to me.

"I'm sorry, Zach," I said as I put the phone to my ear. "It's my fault the police showed up at the Sanctuary. I told Reyes about Orin's knife, since its markings are so similar to the ones on the murder weapon."

"It's never good when the police show up here," Zach said, "but Justine is right, it's not your fault. You're trying to help solve a murder, and Reyes needed to know the knife and the murder weapon might have a connection."

"Thanks for understanding."

"Plus," Zach said, his voice so low I had to press the phone against my ear to catch every word, "none of us trust Orin. Better safe than sorry, right?"

"Right. But we know Orin isn't the killer, because Fiona had the flash the night before he came here."

"That doesn't mean he's not guilty of something else. Maybe it's a good thing for him to know he's under scrutiny. It will keep him in line."

"Maybe." I hung up the phone with a knot in my stomach. Orin wouldn't be happy about the police coming around looking for him, and I hoped very much Reyes hadn't mentioned my name.

Since we needed to wait for Tanner and McCrory to conclude their business, we wandered along the aisles of the store. I was able to get a better look at everything now that the store wasn't crammed with shoppers.

There was a shelf along the back wall with porcelain figurines on it, and I started looking through them. My grandmother had collected similar figurines, and I thought maybe I would spot one I recognized from my childhood visits to her.

As I bent down and reached for a figurine near the back of the bottom shelf, a glint of dull silver caught my eye. There was something made of metal at the very back of the shelf, pressed up against the wall. My fingers wrapped around it, and I pulled it toward me.

When I straightened up, Justine gasped. "Is that what I think it is?"

I held up the silver knife. It looked identical to Orin's, except there was only one symbol inside the scrollwork on the blade. It was the strange quotation mark, like the axe had been inscribed with. "There might not be a secret room, but this was practically hidden," I said.

"We're buying it," Clara announced.

"Why?" I asked.

She blew out a breath. "Because that blade can kill a vampire."

CHAPTER TWENTY-ONE

I nearly dropped the knife in my surprise. "How do you know this can kill a vampire?"

Clara pointed at the symbol that looked like a quotation mark. "That represents fangs."

"Silver can kill vampires, too?" I asked.

"If it's specifically for killing vampires, then it's more than just a silver knife," Justine said. "I've heard some blades are cooled in holy water after they're forged, though Theo says holy water and garlic don't do anything against vampires. Those are just myths."

"And to answer your original question, Olivia," Clara said, "we're buying it because we don't want this falling into the wrong hands. It could be used to kill our friends."

I thought of Mori and Theo, and I wondered how they would react when they found out we had discovered a vampire-slaying knife in the local antique store. "I don't like that all these hunter's weapons are floating around town," I said.

"Believe me, none of us do," Clara said. "I've already told my family to be on high alert. My aunt has even started giving patrons at Under the Undertaker's a pat-down before they're allowed through the door, though she also admitted she's only doing it to the good-looking men who come to the bar."

The price tag said the knife was seventy-five dollars, but Clara was right: we had to buy it to keep anyone else from doing so. The three of us made a thorough search of the other shelves along the back wall, but we didn't find any more hidden weapons.

Wanda looked surprised when I carefully put the knife on the counter in front of her. "I'd like to buy this," I said, "but is there any chance I can get the same discount you gave me earlier?"

"What are you planning to use it for?" Wanda asked warily.

"I have some friends who will want this," I said, thinking of Theo and Mori.

Wanda chewed on her lip as she stared at the knife. "I can't give a discount for high-value items like this."

Orin had said his knife had been cheap because Mrs. Knowles didn't know its real value. Seventy-five didn't seem cheap to me. Then again, I didn't wear a diamond ring, like Orin did. "I understand," I said.

Wanda looked up at me. "Look, I know why you want it. The designs look like what was on the axe that was used to kill Cynthia. You can buy it for seventy-five, or I'll sell it to someone else for an even higher price."

Justine leaned past me, toward Wanda. "You're going to jack up the price because the knife resembles the murder weapon?"

Wanda gave a little shrug. "I have to make a good impression if Tina is going to keep me around."

Justine plopped her purse onto the counter and pulled out her wallet. When I gave her a questioning look, she said, "It's going on the company credit card. I'm sure Damien will understand."

As Wanda rang up the knife, she said, "You're going to display it at your haunted house, aren't you?" She looked pointedly at Clara. "I remember you from when my friends

142

and I went for Halloween. People will love seeing it. Make sure you tell them where it came from."

Once we paid, Wanda smirked at us like she'd just won a battle. *And here I thought we'd bonded over our necklaces earlier.*

"Who needs a supernatural black market when you've got Mining Town Antiques?" I asked sarcastically as soon as we were outside.

"The knife isn't going to fall into dangerous hands," Justine said. "That's all that matters. Now, we just need Tanner and McCrory to—" She cut off as the two of them emerged suddenly from the wall right next to us.

"Let's go!" McCrory shouted.

"We are leaving!" Tanner added.

The ghosts seemed agitated, and they didn't stop to explain as they hurried to my car. I could barely see them in the daylight, but the cold chill they left in their wake was an easy trail to follow. Once we were on the road and heading back toward town, Clara asked them what was going on.

"Ooh, she's mad as a hornet, Mrs. Knowles." McCrory sounded scared.

"Or whatever part of Mrs. Knowles is still in that store," Tanner said. "I'm not sure it's her ghost as much as it is the leftovers of all her anger and judgment. Her essence."

"Almost like a residual haunting," Justine said knowingly. "The bad energy she left behind."

"I guess that means you won't be getting any details from her?" I asked.

"No," Tanner confirmed. "Just blind anger. If it is her ghost, then it's going to take a long time for her to calm down enough that she'll be able to hold a conversation."

"In her defense, she was murdered," McCrory said. "You and I were pretty angry ghosts for the first two decades or so after we killed each other."

"Is that typical?" I asked. "I mean, do murder victims often come back as ghosts?"

"Sure," McCrory said. "Anytime there's a violent death, you have a higher risk of a haunting. A lot of spirits stick around because they're angry or vengeful. Those deep emotions can overcome a ghost's good sense until they learn to control it. I guarantee you'll solve this murder before Mrs. Knowles calms down."

I fell silent, disappointed our scheme of talking to Mrs. Knowles herself hadn't panned out.

Clara must have been thinking the same thing because she said, "But we got the knife, and that's important."

"Knife?" Tanner asked.

We told the ghosts about the knife, which looked like it had been specifically made for a vampire slayer. Justine ended by saying she was going to take it to Damien for safekeeping.

Tanner whistled. "There was nothing like that in the store back when we lived there. Wild."

It wasn't until I pulled into the dirt lot next to the Sanctuary that I looked at the clock on the dash of my car. The family meeting would start in just an hour. I let Clara, Justine, and the ghosts out of the car, then hurried home to scarf down some dinner and get ready for work.

When I got back to the Sanctuary, this time dressed in black jeans and my usual black Sanctuary T-shirt, I was really feeling just how long and adventurous our day had been. I wanted a nap more than anything, but I would have to wait until I got home after work to fall into bed.

I stashed my purse and jacket in my locker, then continued on down the hallway to the dining room. Before I reached the open door, I heard a whoop and knew it was Tanner. Sure enough, I walked in to find him and McCrory standing between two of the tables. They were regaling everyone nearby with an overly dramatic and definitely embellished version of their encounter with Mrs. Knowles.

Theo was already at our usual table, and he leaned over to nudge my arm when I sat down. "You're with me tonight," he said.

"In the lagoon vignette?" I stifled a yawn.

"Seraphina requested you. She says she feels safer knowing you're watching her back."

"Literally." I laughed, since my spot in the vignette was behind Seraphina's tank.

Theo's face sobered. "And I know you're looking out for me, too. Justine and Clara told Mori and me about the knife as soon as we woke up this evening."

"I don't think any of us will feel truly safe until this whole thing is over with."

"We've got Saturday-night crowds already lining up at the door, but when you're not scaring guests, you can conjure some resolution."

"Yes, please," said Mori, who was just walking up to our table. Instead of sitting, she began to pace slowly. Felipe followed at her heels, whimpering.

"Did something happen?" I prompted. I reached down, and Felipe trotted over to me, happy someone was paying attention to him.

Mori stopped pacing and gestured at me as I scratched Felipe behind the ears. "Orin coming here was bad enough. And now, we've got weapons made for killing vampires showing up in the local mom-and-pop store? I don't like it."

"Theo," I said, "I know you said Seraphina requested me, but Mori is all by herself in that hallway after the cemetery vignette. Maybe I should join her."

Mori smiled at me. "That's very sweet of you, but someone has already been assigned to watch over me."

I heard a deep sigh from just behind Mori, and I

leaned to one side to see Damien standing there, looking very unhappy. "I have to wear a costume," he grumbled. "And scare people."

I started laughing, my weariness forgotten. "This is fantastic! I can't wait to see you all dressed up, Damien. Are you going to play a vampire, too?"

Damien threw a look at Mori. "She says I should be her victim."

"All it requires is a little fake blood," Mori said soothingly. "So much easier for you than a full vampire costume. I'm just trying to make this situation as convenient for you as possible."

Mori's tone wasn't convincing anyone. The glee in her eyes was a dead giveaway that she couldn't wait to pretend to suck Damien's blood, time after time, for four hours straight. I figured it was a little payback for what a jerk he'd been when he had first arrived in Nightmare.

Damien had a look that clearly said it was too soon to tease him about his unconventional security duty, so I turned my attention to Felipe instead. I leaned down and planted a kiss on his nose while I tried my hardest not to laugh at Damien's predicament.

After the family meeting, I headed for the costume room. Even once I was changed into my pirate outfit and had put on my makeup, Damien still hadn't shown up to get into his own costume. I really wanted to see his look for the night, but it seemed I would have to track him down inside the haunt to get a peek.

The lagoon vignette had a couple extra people in it when I walked through one of the tunnel doors into the scene a short while later. Fiona was standing at the foot of Seraphina's tank, having a discussion with her, and Mori was chatting with Theo. Felipe was walking a slow circle around Mori.

I walked toward the tank, and Fiona turned to me,

looking a lot less unnerved than she had the last time I had seen her. "All good, I assume?" I asked.

"Orin hasn't come anywhere near Sera," Fiona said. "I think Gunnar is making sure of that."

"Poor guy," Seraphina said. She was leaning over the top edge of the tank, and a few water drops plopped onto the floor in front of me. "Gunnar isn't coming anywhere near me, either. I think he feels really bad about this whole situation. I told him I'm not mad at him."

"He's giving you space," I said. "I'm sure things between you and Gunnar will be fine."

"Just as soon as that tooth fairy is gone."

The overhead lights blinked three times, then stayed off. "Gotta go," Fiona said. She blew a kiss toward Seraphina, then gave my arm a pat. "Thanks for keeping an eye on her, Olivia."

"Of course."

Fiona and Mori disappeared, heading to their spots inside the haunt. I would have to wait until my break time to get a glimpse of Damien in his vampire's victim getup.

The first guests of the evening came into the lagoon vignette about five minutes after the overhead lights had extinguished. As Theo had predicted, it was a busy night, and we had a steady stream of people coming through.

We had only been open for about fifteen minutes when I turned and snarled at someone who was straggling behind his group. He yelped and hustled out of the vignette, and I had to hold in my laughter as I watched him go.

"Olivia," a voice said right into my ear.

I jumped, then rolled my eyes. Theo loved sneaking up on me, and he had waited until my back was turned so I wouldn't see him coming. "You got me," I admitted as I turned to face him.

Except it wasn't Theo. It was Orin, and even in the low

lighting, I could see the way his lips were pulled back, showing off his top and bottom teeth.

Orin's fingers curled around my arms, and he leaned in until our faces were only inches apart. "Are you trying to sabotage me?" he hissed.

CHAPTER TWENTY-TWO

He knows.

As I stared at Orin and that mouth full of teeth, it was all I could think about. Somehow, Orin knew I was the one who had told the police about his knife and his connection to the antique store.

And his connection to the murder.

I forced myself to respond, but my words sounded weak and raspy. "I'm not trying to sabotage anyone."

Orin's fingers tightened around my arms. *Where is Malcolm? Where's Theo?*

"I know you're the one who set the police on me," Orin said. His calm, matter-of-fact tone only added to how scary he was. He felt like a ticking bomb that might explode at any second.

"I didn't set the police on anyone. I told Reyes I'd seen a knife that had similar markings to the ones on the murder weapon." My voice was shaking. "How did you know it was me, anyway?"

Orin's mouth moved into something that resembled a smile. "Your cop friend isn't a good liar. I asked him if he learned about the knife from you, and his denial was obviously untrue. Besides, everyone knows you're the one who always wants to solve the murder and be the hero. Maybe you even killed that woman so you could swoop in and save

149

the day by framing me for it. Everyone would praise you while I sat in jail for something you did. Maybe you're behind all the murders in this town."

Before I could even form a response to such an accusation, Orin's face abruptly jerked away from mine. I caught sight of hands gripping his shoulders as he was hauled backward. Damien's face appeared next to Orin's, his eyes glowing bright green in the darkness of the vignette.

Damien said something into Orin's ear, then released him. Orin's smug look disappeared, and he turned toward the entrance to the tunnels without looking at me again. I saw Malcolm fall into step behind him.

Without a word, Damien took my hand and followed Malcolm. But, when Malcolm trailed Orin into a tunnel that turned left, Damien kept going straight, leading us to a back hallway that connected the tunnels with the staff-only east wing of the Sanctuary.

Damien didn't say anything until we were in his office, the door shut and locked behind us. I noticed he was still dressed in the black trousers and pale-blue shirt he had been wearing during the family meeting, rather than a costume.

When Damien spoke, his voice was tight. "Gunnar came to me right after the family meeting and said he couldn't find Orin. We've been searching everywhere. I pulled Malcolm from the lagoon vignette because I figured Seraphina was safe there. It never occurred to me Orin would go after you."

"Orin must have waited in the shadows until he knew Theo was distracted by guests." My voice was stronger now that I was in the safety of Damien's office—and Damien's presence, for that matter. I took off my tricorn pirate hat and threw it onto one of the chairs, then ran shaking fingers through my hair.

Damien's hand gripped the mantel above the fireplace,

and his jaw muscles flexed. "This is my fault," he said quietly. "I asked you to investigate the murder, and now you're in danger because of it."

"Lucky for me you were there to rescue me," I said. "How did you happen to be in the lagoon vignette right at that moment, anyway?"

"Tanner and McCrory were helping us search for Orin. They told me what you went through today at the antique store. I wanted to make sure you were doing okay, so Malcolm and I went to the lagoon vignette to check on you. We got there and found Orin looking like he was going to devour you in one bite."

"The ghosts like to embellish. It was a wild day at the antique store, but nothing dangerous. Still, I'm really glad you showed up when you did."

Damien's shoulders lowered a couple inches as he began to relax. "I just don't want you to get hurt."

"I don't think that will happen. Orin would have to get through you and everyone else at the Sanctuary first."

"He almost did. Olivia, if you're not already, I want you to work on conjuring your safety. Instead of using your ability to get clues to the murder, I want you to focus on staying safe."

I quirked an eyebrow at Damien. "Maybe I already did conjure my safety. You showed up right as Orin was confronting me, because in the middle of your search for him, you suddenly felt the need to check on me."

"Thanks to the ghosts and their storytelling," Damien said thoughtfully. "Even still, you might be right."

A sudden thought struck me, and I gasped. "Oh, no. What if I did this?"

"Did what?" Damien asked. "Make Orin confront you?"

"No. The murder. Reyes has said there weren't this

many murders before I came to Nightmare. What if I'm conjuring them?"

Damien looked at me with slightly narrowed eyes. At least their bright glow had dulled to a smolder. "You're worried you might be conjuring all the murders in Nightmare?"

"Orin said maybe I was the one who killed Mrs. Knowles, so I could frame him and look like the hero. He said everyone knows I love solving murders, and maybe I'm the one responsible for all of them." My breath hitched, and the words began to roll together. "Maybe I do secretly love the thrill of solving a murder. Maybe I'm conjuring all these dead bodies because it makes me feel good to find the killer. I'm subconsciously creating the crimes so I can solve them."

Damien moved closer to me and wrapped his hands around my arms. It had hurt when Orin did it, but Damien's touch was gentle and reassuring. "You know that's not true," he said firmly. "Orin put you on edge, and now he's trying to play mind games with you. That's all it is."

I felt a tear slide down my cheek. "But what if I am responsible? What if I've been conjuring for years, before I ever knew I had any supernatural ability? Right after I met you, you asked me if I always got what I wanted. I laughed at you, because I was divorced and had no money, and I had broken down in Nightmare on my way to starting a new life. But what if I conjured all of that? What if I conjured my divorce, then somehow made my car break down right outside this town?"

"What if you did?" Damien asked. "Aren't you happier now?"

I blinked at Damien. What if I *had* conjured everything that had led to me being in Nightmare? Had I turned my own life upside down? "I can't remember the last time I was this happy," I admitted.

"Then it doesn't matter *how* you wound up here. It just matters that you *are* here. You were meant to come to Nightmare, Olivia. And so was I." Damien stepped so close to me I had to look up to keep my eyes on his.

"Neither one of us was happy with our old lives," Damien continued softly. His head tilted down, and his eyes flashed green. "Here, though…"

Damien trailed off as his eyes closed, and his lips found mine. His kiss was warm and soft, and after my initial surprise, I relaxed and leaned into him. My arms slid around his waist as one of his hands lifted to my hair.

It is like that, my brain thought lazily as the kiss deepened.

I was so engrossed in the moment that I almost didn't register the noise. It started quietly, like someone tapping their fingers against a hard surface, then rapidly rose to a thrumming. The sound died as quickly as it had begun, and there was a brief moment of silence followed by a crashing *thud* that seemed to come from all around us.

Damien and I pulled away from each other at the same time. His eyes were still glowing as he glanced down to his right. I followed his gaze and saw a pile of books next to us. There was another pile beside it and another after that.

I swiveled my head around. Every single book had flown off the shelves, and they were piled in a perfect circle around Damien and me.

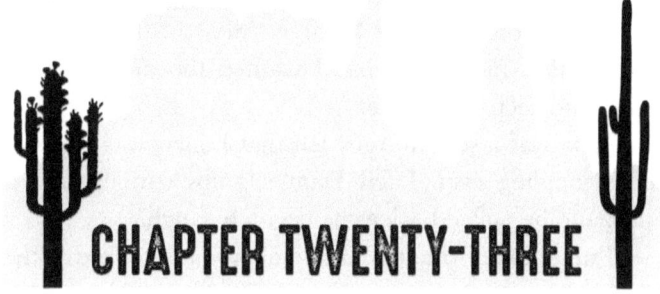

CHAPTER TWENTY-THREE

I slid my arms from around Damien's waist and clapped my hands together. "Damien, this is incredible! Look what you did!"

Damien was looking at the books, his face a mixture of astonishment and excitement. "But how? I'm not angry or upset."

I laughed. "Don't you see? We've known for months now that your psychic power unleashes when your emotions are heightened, but we assumed that meant negative emotions. We've been waiting until you're upset to practice controlling your ability, but it turns out positive emotions are just as powerful."

Damien looked at the circle of books. "Maybe even more powerful. Possibly easier to control, as well. I wasn't even trying to do this, but look how the books are stacked so neatly around us."

"I know! This is so exciting!"

"Want to try putting the books back on the shelves?" Damien asked slyly. He was smiling down at me, his arms already pulling me close to him again. "You can conjure my control so they all fly back into place."

I tilted my head up and lifted my heels slightly off the floor, and Damien's second kiss felt every bit as good as the first.

I tried to conjure. Really, I did. But it was hard to focus on books when I was being kissed. Plus, conjuring required me to focus on the thing I wanted most in the moment. And, in that moment, what I wanted the most was for Damien to keep kissing me.

There was a sound to my left that I knew was a pile of books toppling over. I felt Damien's lips curl up into a smile, and he pulled back as he began to laugh.

"I'm a little distracted," I said as we both looked at the books that were now scattered across the floor.

"We should have done this sooner. I might have made a lot of progress in my skills by now."

"Better late than never?" I asked.

Damien smiled and ran his fingers along my jawline. "I've wanted to kiss you since before Halloween. I just didn't know if you wanted it, too." He dropped his hand and looked at the books again. "I guess we'll have to put these back on the shelves the old-fashioned way."

I was just reaching down to grab a handful of books when there was a knock on the door. Damien hopped over a stack of books to answer it.

"Hey," Zach said, stepping past Damien into the office. He eyed the books, then looked warily at Damien. "I can come back later."

"I'm not upset," Damien said.

Zach looked at the books again. "But you did this with your mind, right?"

"I did. Without being angry in the slightest. As it turns out, my power is enhanced when I'm happy, too."

A grin slowly spread over Zach's face as his eyes moved between Damien and me. "I knew it," he said. He pumped a fist. "I knew it! I was right!"

"Right about what?" I asked innocently.

"I just won fifty bucks!" Zach said, ignoring my question.

"What? How?"

Zach planted his hands on his hips, his chest puffed out proudly. "I won the pool. Everyone put in a few bucks and picked a week on the calendar. And I won."

Damien tried to give Zach a stern look but completely failed. "There's a Sanctuary betting pool about when Olivia and I would finally...?"

"Finally stop ignoring the fact you two like each other," Zach finished. "Mori tried to claim she won when you two were holding hands a few weeks ago, but I told her Olivia was just trying to help you control your power, and she has to maintain contact with you to do it. But I can tell by the looks on your faces that whatever you were doing in here just now was more than *practice*." Zach made air quotes with his fingers on the last word.

Damien was still trying to look like he didn't find the betting pool funny at all, but when I burst out laughing, he finally relented and joined in.

After a few moments, Zach said, "I actually came to say that Malcolm followed Orin all the way to the saloon."

I frowned. "Not to Under the Undertaker's? Why would Orin go to the saloon rather than a bar for supernatural creatures?"

Zach shrugged. "Maybe he likes hanging around with humans more than us. Who knows? Either way, Malcolm said Orin is acting shady. He keeps looking around, like he's afraid he's being followed."

"He is being followed," I pointed out.

"True. Either way, I thought maybe we could make it a group outing. Malcolm is going to draw a lot of attention if he goes into the saloon by himself."

"Who's covering the ticket window?" Damien asked.

"Justine. So we don't need to pull anyone from the vignettes."

"Good." Damien reached a hand toward me. "Can I buy you a drink?"

"That would be nice. Thank you," I said sweetly, taking his hand and carefully stepping over the books. "We can clean this mess up later."

"Let's go out the back," Damien suggested. We looped past the queue in the entryway and headed into the back hallway, then went out the back door. That let us avoid all the people waiting in the ticket line out front.

Damien volunteered to drive, and as we headed toward High Noon Boulevard, I glanced at my watch. "How did Orin get to the saloon so quickly? It was only minutes from the time he was looming over me in the lagoon vignette to the time he was at the saloon."

"Tooth fairies can move fast," Zach noted. "Good thing Malcolm is even faster, so Orin couldn't shake him."

If I walked from the Sanctuary to the saloon, it would take me at least fifteen minutes. Orin had done it in a much shorter amount of time, which meant his supernatural speed was impressive.

It was also scary. No wonder he had been able to sneak up on me so easily.

High Noon Boulevard was the hub of tourist activity in Nightmare, and the street was closed to traffic. Instead, the paved road had been covered with dirt, and during the day, horse-drawn stagecoaches gave tourists rides up and down its length. Several times a day, actors portraying Tanner and McCrory recreated the legendary shootout in the middle of the street.

Saturday nights could be especially crowded on High Noon Boulevard, because tourists flocked to the Nightmare Saloon, which had been restored to look like it was from the mining boom years in the late eighteen hundreds. The entrance even had short swinging doors, and an upright piano in one corner sounded tinny and old-fashioned.

The streets nearest High Noon Boulevard were lined with parked cars, so we had to park farther away, then walk a bit to get to the saloon.

I didn't mind, though. Damien held my hand the entire way, and other than Zach giggling at the sight and telling us how he was going to spend his fifty bucks, it was a nice walk.

Malcolm had texted Zach that he was at a table in the front right corner of the saloon. We had to thread our way through the crowd to reach him. Zach had been right that Malcolm would draw too much attention if he was sitting by himself. People nearby were eyeing him nervously, and a few were openly staring. Zach and Damien looked completely normal, so they would help Malcolm blend in.

I, on the other hand, was still dressed as a pirate, except for the hat I had abandoned in Damien's office. Given that the saloon staff were in costumes, too, no one really seemed to care that I looked like I should be making someone walk the plank.

"Has he spotted you?" I asked Malcolm.

"Not yet. The crowd is helping." Malcolm gestured toward the long wooden bar against the back wall. "He's sitting at the far end of the bar, talking to someone. I think they're having some kind of meeting, because it doesn't look like a casual chat."

I leaned from one side to the other, trying to get a glimpse of Orin and his companion. If he was meeting up with someone who wasn't supernatural, then that explained why he was at the saloon instead of Under the Undertaker's.

Finally, I caught sight of Orin's face, profiled against the mirror that ran along the back wall behind the bar. He was leaning close to the person sitting on the stool to his right, and I was sharply reminded of how it had felt to see his face so close to mine earlier in the evening.

159

I leaned some more, and the person next to him came into view. It was a man wearing a black polo shirt and khaki pants, and his face was partially visible as he turned toward Orin. The man's hair was brown, and I knew that if I was closer to him, I'd be able to see gray streaks running through it.

"I know that man," I said.

Damien was also trying to get a clear view. "He's familiar, but I can't place him."

"He's familiar because he was at the Chamber of Commerce mixer yesterday," I said. "Orin is having a meeting with Bryce Bonner, the accountant who told me how much he disliked Cynthia Knowles."

CHAPTER TWENTY-FOUR

"Do you think the accountant killed Mrs. Knowles?" Zach asked. There was a hint of teasing in his voice, since he himself was an accountant, and I had once suspected him of murder.

"Bryce brought up the murder when we chatted during the mixer," I explained. "He said something about his mother, and how she wouldn't miss Mrs. Knowles. He also mentioned Mrs. Knowles was good at getting people to sell their antiques to her for way less than they were worth."

"That doesn't seem like a motive for murder," Malcolm pointed out.

"True. But there might be more to the story." The tourists standing between our table and the bar moved a bit, and Bryce disappeared from my view.

"Orin isn't causing any trouble," Damien said, "so I think we should leave him alone. We'll stay here and keep watch, but there's no need for us to interrupt him."

"I'm not anxious to be in his company again any time soon," I pointed out.

"Olivia, I need to apologize to you about that," Malcolm said. "I should have been there to protect you tonight."

I shrugged. "None of us thought I needed to be

protected. And don't worry, Orin didn't try to do anything other than scare me."

With nothing to do but watch, we went ahead and ordered a pitcher of beer for the table. It was strange not being at the Sanctuary when it was one of my nights to work. Theo was probably worried since I had disappeared, and I hoped Justine would send someone to let him know everything was okay.

In fact, I realized, I could take care of that myself. I texted Clara, who usually roamed around to give people breaks throughout the night. *I'll explain later, but everything is good,* I typed. *Can you please tell my fellow pirates that I'm doing a little sleuthing and will be back later?*

Less than a minute after I sent the text, my phone buzzed. Clara had responded with a short *On it!*

Damien pulled out his phone, too, as our pitcher of beer arrived. Malcolm was filling our four glasses when Damien pushed his phone toward me. "We'll get some answers tomorrow," he said confidently.

I looked at the phone and saw Damien had found a social media account for Bryce's business, Nightmare Taxes. The latest entry was from just a few hours earlier. *Great day at my son's baseball tournament,* it read. *Can't wait for tomorrow's semifinals. Go Lions!*

"We're going to a youth baseball tournament tomorrow?" I asked.

"Of course. The Sanctuary is a big community supporter." Damien winked at me. "And maybe we'll bump into Bryce while we're there."

I liked that plan. We'd get to talk to Bryce without Orin anywhere nearby.

"You know," I said thoughtfully, "I was trying to conjure more clues yesterday when Bryce came up and started a conversation with me. I thought my conjuring had failed, because our chat didn't turn up any interesting information. But, maybe I did conjure him coming to talk to me, and I didn't realize the significance of it."

"I just want to know how a totally normal, not-at-all-magical accountant knows Orin," Damien said.

"Especially when Orin has only been in town for a few days," Zach pointed out. "I don't think Orin went to the guy for help paying his taxes."

"And I'm guessing Bryce wouldn't recognize a supernatural creature if it jumped up and bit him in the throat," I added. "If he catches a glimpse of Orin's teeth, he's going to have a lot of questions."

After that, we tried our best to enjoy our drinks and each other's company. Zach was refilling his glass when he said casually to Malcolm, "I won fifty dollars tonight."

"Oh, boy," I groaned. "Here we go."

Malcolm looked at me, his face passive. "What a shame. If you had waited just two more weeks, I would have won."

"You were in on the bet, too?" Damien asked.

"Most of us were participating," Malcolm said. He didn't seem at all abashed.

Damien waved his glass in the air. "Maybe I should ask Justine to make an announcement at the family meeting tomorrow night."

"And what exactly would she say?" Zach asked, propping his elbows on the table and resting his chin in his hands. He looked at Damien with both eyebrows raised. "Are you two dating? Keeping it casual? Just scheduling make-out sessions in your office while the rest of us are working the haunt?"

"We were not making out!" I sputtered.

"Well, if Zach hadn't interrupted us…"

"Damien!" I didn't know whether I wanted to laugh or crawl under the table and hide.

Malcolm, Zach, and even Damien all started to laugh.

It had been so long since I had shared a first kiss with someone, and something told me the entire staff of the Sanctuary would know about it by midnight.

Orin and Bryce continued to sit at the bar for about another thirty minutes, then Orin threaded his way through the crowd and out through the swinging doors. If he had spotted us, he didn't give any indication of it. He didn't glance our way once as he was leaving.

"We could go talk to Bryce now," I said once Orin was gone. I was so ready to dive into questioning that I was already halfway out of my seat when I felt Damien's fingers around my wrist.

"Too late," he said.

He was right. When I caught a glimpse of Bryce through a break in the crowd, I saw him pulling on a windbreaker, clearly getting ready to leave. I sat back down, and we wrapped up our drinks and our conversation before calling it a night. Malcolm and Zach wanted to get back to the Sanctuary since that was probably where Orin had gone, and I was ready for bed.

Damien drove me home, and instead of letting me out of his car at the foot of my stairs, as usual, he parked and walked me up to my door. At first, I found it sweet, but by the time I had my key in the lock, I was feeling nervous. *Am I supposed to ask him in? Is that too forward? I don't want him to get the wrong idea. What should I do?*

I had forgotten how stressful dating could be.

I opened my door and turned to Damien, still unsure what I was supposed to do or say. He seemed to sense my hesitation, because he gave me a little smile. "It's going to take some getting used to, isn't it?"

"Yeah. It's been a long time since I've done any of this."

"We'll figure it out together." Damien had been engaged before he returned to Nightmare, so it had probably been a while since he had gone through the experience of dating someone new, too.

Damien raised his hand to my cheek, then leaned forward and kissed me softly. When he pulled back and looked at me, his eyes were glowing faintly. "Good night, Olivia."

"Good night, Damien." I stood in the open doorway and watched until Damien had pulled out of the motel's parking lot, then I sighed and shut the door.

After the day's events, I had expected sleep to be elusive. Instead, I drifted off almost as soon as I crawled under the covers, and I slept peacefully.

The next morning, I turned off my alarm when it buzzed and let myself sleep in. I was finally up and having my first cup of coffee when Mama called me.

"We're having a girls' brunch," she said. "Would you like to join us?"

"Sure," I agreed.

"Great. Come up to the office in thirty minutes, and I'll drive."

Thirty minutes wasn't a lot of time, so I shot out of my chair and hustled to shower and get ready. I made it up to the office with a minute to spare, dressed in a lavender floral-print dress with a gray cardigan to guard against the chill.

When I walked into the motel office, Benny and Mama were standing behind the counter. "There she is," Mama said happily. "Well, we're off. Thanks for watching the desk, dear." Mama gave her husband a kiss on the cheek.

"You girls stay out of trouble," Benny said, grinning in my direction.

Mama was wearing a dress, too, but hers was a long burgundy number that swirled down to her ankles. "How fancy is this place?" I asked as we walked out the door.

"It's not," she answered. "When I woke up this morning, I had a sense that something good had happened. Something to celebrate. So, I thought I would dress for the occasion."

"Oh. What happened?"

We had reached Mama's car, and she laughed as she opened the driver's side door of her red vintage Mustang. "You can tell me while we drive."

Mama climbed in, then reached across to unlock my door. I got in slowly, trying to figure out how to respond to that comment. I eventually went with, "What makes you think the celebratory event has to do with me?"

"Your vibe is like a bright golden light this morning. You're happy about something."

Mama started the car, the engine roaring to life, but then she put her hands in her lap and looked at me expectantly. "We're not going to brunch until you spill the beans."

I rubbed the back of my neck and stared out the windshield. "Well. Last night… Um." I glanced at Mama, who looked like she was going to start laughing at my discomfort. "We've known for months that Damien's powers spike when his emotions spike."

"Huh," Mama said, her mirth barely contained. "So this has to do with Damien, then?"

"We found out last night that any kind of strong emotions make his power manifest. We've been focusing on him getting angry or upset, but as it turns out, he can unleash his power when he's very happy, too. Your feeling this morning was correct: we do have something to celebrate. This is a huge step for him."

Mama continued to stare me down, and I realized there was no point trying to hide the truth from someone with her supernatural perception. "He rearranged every single book in his office with his psychic power." I cleared my throat, then quickly added, "When he kissed me."

"Yes!" Mama shouted. She pressed her palm into the horn and let off three blasts. "I knew it! You had a look on your face when you walked in this morning, and I thought, *Oh, he finally did it.*"

Mama didn't ask for a blow-by-blow account of my evening, even though she looked like she wanted to. Instead, she steered us out onto the road, humming happily to herself.

As we drove, Mama told me we were heading for a restaurant called The Parlor. "It's in a former funeral parlor," Mama said. "But don't worry. You'd never know to look at the place that it used to be for corpses instead of cappuccinos."

She was right. We pulled into the parking lot about five minutes later, and the place looked more like a house than a former funeral parlor. There was a covered front porch supported by tall white columns, and the white clapboard facade was the perfect backdrop for the riot of purple, pink, and yellow flowers growing from planters set across the entire front of the building.

The inside was just as charming, with lots of plants, floral tablecloths, and plenty of sunshine coming through tall windows. It felt slightly frilly, like we should be going there to drink afternoon tea with our pinkies sticking out.

In the midst of the elegance was Lucy, who was standing near the front with her mom, Mia. I had never seen Lucy in a dress before, and I wasn't surprised it was pink. Mia had tamed Lucy's curls into two French braids.

I hadn't seen Mia in a while, since her busy schedule as a hairdresser often clashed with my own work schedule, so I happily greeted her and Lucy.

We were seated at a round table right next to one of the windows. Mama waited until we had ordered before she blurted, "Olivia is dating Damien."

"Oh, how sweet," Mia said. "I could tell he liked you when you two joined us for Thanksgiving dinner."

Lucy's reaction was much stronger than her mother's. "Can I be the flower girl at your wedding?" she asked, bouncing in her seat.

"We're not getting married," I clarified.

"Not yet, maybe," Mama said under her breath.

By the time our food arrived, the conversation had moved on, and I was halfway through my eggs Benedict when Mia mentioned the murder. "I've been hearing about nothing else from my clients. Every single one of them had something bad to say about Mrs. Knowles."

"Damien and I are going to chat with an accountant named Bryce Bonner this afternoon," I said. "He mentioned something about his mother not liking Mrs. Knowles, and we think he might have helpful information about who would have had a good reason to kill her."

"Bryce himself has a good reason," Mama said without hesitation. "His mother had every right to despise Mrs. Knowles. Mrs. Bonner got such a bad deal at the antique store that it was practically robbery, and to make it worse, it was all her husband's keepsakes that she sold after his death. The Bonners have held a grudge against Mrs. Knowles for years. For them, it's personal."

CHAPTER TWENTY-FIVE

"Bryce mentioned that Mrs. Knowles would convince people to sell things to her for far less than they were worth, but he didn't tell me those details," I said. "No wonder he's not sorry Mrs. Knowles is gone."

Mama nodded. "Apparently, Mrs. Bonner really needed the money, or she never would have sold off her husband's things. Mrs. Knowles made her feel like she was getting a good deal, but later, after Bryce found the old receipts from when Mr. Bonner bought the items, they realized they should have held out for more money."

"And they couldn't buy those things back from Mrs. Knowles," I guessed.

"Mrs. Bonner tried," Mia said. "She used to come to our salon, and she told all of us how she went back to the antique store and told Mrs. Knowles she'd made a mistake. Mrs. Knowles said she knew exactly what she had done, and it was Mrs. Bonner's fault for not doing her research beforehand. She had zero sympathy for a woman who was still grieving her husband's death."

Suddenly, Bryce's meeting with Orin at the saloon was making a lot more sense. Bryce didn't seem like the type to commit murder, but it was entirely possible he had hired someone to teach Mrs. Knowles a lesson. A deadly, brutal lesson.

I didn't want to present my theory during our brunch, especially since Lucy was there. Brunch seemed like a place for happier topics. We wrapped up, and Mama and I got back to the motel just a few minutes before Damien called to say he was on his way to pick me up so we could go talk to Bryce at the baseball tournament.

Boy, are we going to have a lot of questions for him.

I had just enough time to change into jeans and a blue shirt, though I kept the gray cardigan as part of the ensemble. The sun was shining, but the breeze kept the day from feeling warm.

I was halfway down my stairs when Damien pulled up. When I got into the passenger seat, he reached over, took my hand, and brought it to his lips. "Hi."

I could get used to this.

"I hate to ruin the mood," I said, "but Mama and Mia had some interesting things to say about Bryce Bonner and his mom." As we drove, I filled Damien in on what I'd learned during brunch.

"I'm glad we're talking to Bryce today, then," Damien said when I was finished. "And I'm really glad we didn't confront him or Orin last night. You know, Fiona said Orin couldn't have killed Mrs. Knowles, because she got the flash on Wednesday night, and Orin didn't arrive in Nightmare until Thursday morning. But what if Bryce made the decision to kill Mrs. Knowles before Orin ever got to town? He may not have known how he would do it, or if he would hire someone to do it for him, but his determination to kill her might have sparked Fiona's forewarning of death."

"Which means Orin might have killed Mrs. Knowles on Bryce's orders." I nodded. "I was also thinking that was a possibility, and that timeline fits with Fiona's information."

Nightmare's sports complex was near the high school,

and we arrived to find baseball games happening on each of the three diamonds in the complex. We were heading for the nearest one in our search for Bryce, when I heard someone calling my name.

I turned to see Madge and Morgan walking toward us. Madge was dressed in a red blouse and slim gray trousers, looking very modern as well as very pretty. Morgan was in her usual long black dress, which looked like it had been out of fashion for more than a century. She looked so out of place that people were turning to stare at her as she passed them.

"Hi, ladies," I said, surprised. "We didn't expect to see you two here."

"And we didn't expect to see you," Morgan said.

"We had no premonition of it," Madge added. "It is truly a surprise, which doesn't happen often to a witch."

"Where's Maida?" I asked, looking back in the direction Madge and Morgan had come from.

"Watching the game," Madge said. "She loves baseball, so we thought she would enjoy the tournament."

I certainly hadn't expected the youngest witch to be a baseball fan—or a fan of any sport, for that matter—and I had to shake my head at my biased assumption. Maida was, despite being a witch and wise beyond her years, still just a kid at heart. So what if she wore pointy-toed black boots and worked magic? She could still love watching baseball.

"Maybe we should have a friendly little game at the Sanctuary one night after work," Damien suggested. "I played some in middle school."

"Oh, she would love that," Morgan said.

"We would just have to keep her from putting a hex on the opposing team," Madge said thoughtfully.

"I'll be the scorekeeper," I volunteered. "I don't need to be hexed to be terrible at sports."

"We'll see you ladies later," Damien said, sliding his hand into mine. "Olivia and I are looking for someone who might have information about the murder."

"You two are getting close," Morgan said, a small smile on her lips.

"I hope so," I responded. "The man we're looking for might know who killed Mrs. Knowles."

Madge laughed. "She didn't mean you're getting close to solving the murder, though I'm sure you are. She meant close to each other. If you two had started dating between Christmas and New Year's, I would have made fifty dollars!"

"No one told me there was a schedule to stick to," I said lightly as Damien and I began walking. Morgan's cackle followed us as we headed toward the nearest baseball diamond.

As we got closer, we could see that neither of the teams playing was called the Lions, so we moved on to the next game. It was quickly apparent we were in the right place because the kids stationed at the bases had red lion heads on the fronts of their jerseys.

"There he is," Damien said a moment later, pointing with his free hand. Sure enough, Bryce Bonner was standing to one side of the concession stand, a soda, a hot dog, and a red-and-white-striped box of popcorn balanced in his hands.

"And there's Wanda!" I nearly shouted in my surprise. She was standing next to Bryce, facing him with her arms crossed over her chest. She was turned away from us just enough that I couldn't see her facial expression, but judging by her stiff body language, she was upset.

Damien and I walked up behind Wanda quietly. I didn't need to tell Damien that I hoped to overhear some of the conversation. Our stealth was rewarded, because when I got closer, I heard Wanda say, "I'm telling you, it's all gone."

Oh, she's angry.

"Who bought the axe, then?" Bryce asked. His voice was tight, but I couldn't tell if he was angry, like Wanda, or scared.

"Don't you think the police already asked me that? No one bought it! It was stolen."

Bryce was squeezing the popcorn box so hard that pieces were spilling out of the top and onto the ground. "I told you she was an awful woman, and I can't say I'm sad it was my father's axe that killed her."

I gasped before I could stop myself, and Wanda whirled around. "You again," she said, eyeing me like I might have been the one who stole the axe.

Bryce tried to smile at us, but it only made him look like he was in mild pain. "Olivia, right? And Damien. Good to see you both."

"The axe Mrs. Knowles was killed with belonged to your dad?" I asked. I probably should have started with hello, but I felt like I was close to getting some answers, so I didn't want to waste time with pleasantries.

Bryce shrugged, the motion spilling more of his popcorn. "It was part of my dad's collection of occult items. After he died, my mom needed money to pay for all of his medical bills and the funeral, so she sold most of the pieces to the antique store."

"And Mrs. Knowles paid her a fraction of what the pieces were worth," I said.

"Yeah. There was a lot in the collection, too. A pair of silver knives, a sword, a crossbow, chalices, a bowl… Every piece was covered in a bunch of occult symbols."

I didn't bother to tell Bryce the weapons were decorated with hunter's symbols rather than occult ones. He was probably picturing the knives and other items being used in rituals, like spell casting, not being used on people like my friends at the Sanctuary.

"I've seen the knives," I said.

"You bought one of them yesterday," Wanda pointed out.

"How funny," Bryce said. "The other knife was just sold on Wednesday."

"Thursday," Damien corrected him. "A, uh, colleague of ours bought it on Thursday morning."

Bryce shook his head. "No, Orin bought the knife on Wednesday. He loved it so much that he asked Mrs. Knowles if she had any more like it, but she couldn't find the other knife. Orin talked her into giving him my phone number, so he could ask about anything my mom might have held onto and passed on to me. He called me that night."

"You and Orin spoke on Wednesday night?" I asked.

Bryce nodded. "Yes. And when you saw us at the saloon last night, we were closing a deal for him to buy a gun my father had owned."

So much for us flying under the radar last night.

I felt Damien's fingers twitch. "What kind of gun?"

"An old six-shooter with the same kind of filigree design and occult symbols on it as the other pieces. It came with a box of bullets that Orin said are really rare."

Because they had a high silver content, I was sure. I wasn't as interested in the deal that had been happening on Saturday night. Rather, I was still thinking about that phone call Orin had made on Wednesday. He had arrived in Nightmare a day before he claimed he had, and he had talked to someone with a grudge against Mrs. Knowles.

Had Fiona's flash that someone's death was imminent come at the same time Orin and Bryce had been chatting on the phone?

There was something else that was bothering me, too.

"Wanda," I said, "when did you notice the axe had gone missing?"

"I didn't know it had gone missing until the police showed up and started asking questions about it. It's not safe for the pieces from that collection to be out where just anyone can pick them up. They were supposed to be locked away."

"You think they're dangerous?" I asked. There had been other knives on display at the antique store, so I wondered why Wanda thought the knives Orin and I had bought were different.

"Of course they're dangerous," Wanda said, looking at me like I was slightly stupid. "I don't know what kind of rituals they were made for, but they could be used to unleash very powerful magic."

They could be used to unleash death and destruction on my friends. Still, even if Wanda's reasoning were incorrect, I agreed with her on one point. "You're right. They should have been locked up. If only there was a secret occult room they could have been secured in."

Wanda barked out a laugh. "I'm the one who fueled that rumor, you know. When I began working at the antique store, I remembered the story about the secret occult room. I would tell customers about it as a joke, but most of them believed me. People got excited by the idea, and it was good for business, so I started posting about it online. The story took off."

"Where were these items stored, then, if they weren't somewhere secure?" I thought of the knife I had found, practically hidden at the back of a bottom shelf. Had the axe been sitting on a shelf, too, where anyone could have grabbed it?

One of Wanda's shoulders hitched up in a half-hearted shrug. "There might not be a secret room, but there is a secret vault."

CHAPTER TWENTY-SIX

"Actually," Wanda continued, "the vault isn't really secret. It's right out there in the open, but no one suspects it's where the store's valuable items are stored."

"There really is a secret occult vault at the antique store?" Damien asked.

"There's an antique safe on display behind the checkout counter," Wanda explained. "It has a sign on it that says it isn't for sale, with a few sentences about its history. The safe was used by the Nightmare General Store back when this was a Wild West town. Allegedly, that famous outlaw Butch Tanner once tried to break into it."

I'll have to ask Tanner about that. In the meantime, I was more interested in the stolen axe. "The knife I found was sitting on a shelf, so it wasn't secured in the safe."

"Cynthia would sometimes pull those weapons out of the safe and display them. I always told her it was danger-ous, but she wouldn't listen. She never understood their true value, or how dangerous they could be in the wrong hands." Wanda shook her head. "She was the only one who knew the combination to the safe, and there were other valuable items inside it. Nice jewelry, even."

"Surely Mrs. Knowles wrote the combination down somewhere, or told at least one person what it was," I said incredulously. Even though the woman hadn't anticipated getting murdered, it still seemed shortsighted not to have had the combination stored somewhere.

"I once heard her sister ask for the combination, but Cynthia just said, 'I'll tell you later.'" Wanda made a noise that was part laugh, part exasperated sigh.

"You seem to know the value of those items," Bryce said bitterly. "Too bad you weren't the one my mother sold them to."

"A silver knife like the one she got"—Wanda pointed a finger toward me—"could get as much as five hundred dollars."

"Five hundred? The price tag said seventy-five dollars!" If there was any truth to what Wanda was telling me, then Mrs. Bonner really had been cheated out of a good deal. And if one knife could have brought Mrs. Bonner that much money, then the entire collection had probably been worth thousands more than what Mrs. Knowles had paid for it. No wonder Bryce held a grudge.

"Sure," Wanda said. "You can get a lot of money for items like that knife, if you have the right audience. A practitioner of the craft would recognize the value."

My eyes flicked to Wanda's pentagram necklace. "And by the right audience, you mean other witches."

"Witches and those with an interest in the occult." Wanda nodded. "People who would take proper care of these items and not let them fall into the wrong hands."

"Just how many people like that come through the antique store?" Damien asked.

"Not many," Wanda conceded. "But I do the online sales for the store. It's easy to find the right community of buyers that way."

"And the rumor of the secret occult room probably gets those right buyers to come into the store when they visit Nightmare," I guessed.

Wanda nodded, looking proud of herself. "Yes. And

even though they don't find the room, many of them still wind up buying something."

I peered at Wanda. "You said the people you wanted to sell these weapons to would take proper care of them. Do you think Orin will take care of the knife he bought?"

Wanda's face clouded over. "I wouldn't know. Cynthia sold it to him while I was in the back, taking care of online orders. I only briefly met him when he came back to the store yesterday. He said he was just looking around, but there was something about him that put me on my guard."

"You mean his teeth?" Bryce asked. "They look like something you'd see on a monster in a horror movie. I only caught a glimpse, but…" Bryce trailed off, and he shuddered.

"I didn't notice," Wanda said. "It was everything else about him that bothered me. The way he looked at me. The way he moved. Even the way he felt, if you know what I mean."

"His vibe," I said, thinking of Mama.

"Yeah. He gave me the creeps. I don't know what he's going to do with that knife, but it's not going to be anything good. Someone like you,"—Wanda gestured toward me again—"would use it to work good magic. You don't seem like the type to use it for revenge spells or anything bad like that. This guy Orin, though? He's probably already summoned a horde of demons with that knife."

It felt like my brain was trying to put together a jigsaw puzzle, but I was missing a few pieces. There was something significant that I was so close to figuring out, but it was just out of my grasp. All this talk about the safe and the hunter's weapons was pointing me to a meaningful clue, but no matter how hard I tried to pin it down, it eluded me. The information was buried in the conversation, too hidden for me to find.

Hidden. I remembered the flash of silver I had seen when I had crouched down to look at that bottom shelf against the back wall of the store. The way the knife could only be seen by someone who was looking with intent.

"That knife I found," I said slowly, as the thing I had been trying so hard to piece together finally became a clear picture, "it wasn't on display. It wasn't out where someone would instantly notice it. It was hidden at the back of the shelf, like someone didn't want it to be found. You put it there, didn't you?"

Wanda's jaw worked, clenching and unclenching. After a few moments, she spat, "At least I didn't steal it. I left it there in the store. Cynthia had put it on display, and I came in one day to find her about to sell it to a teenager. Occult item or not, she should have been more responsible than to sell a knife to a kid! The next day, I moved the knife somewhere less conspicuous, and Cynthia never noticed. I kept moving it, making it less easy to find, until it was so well hidden, I was convinced no one would find it. I underestimated your determination."

"Why didn't you just put it back into the safe?" I asked.

"Because Cynthia would have taken it right back out again. I tried the same thing with the other knife, and it didn't work. She put it on display when I wasn't there, and then she let that weird guy buy it."

"If you put the other knife in the safe," I said, "then that means you must have known the combination."

Wanda sucked in her breath, and her face paled. Her eyes darted between me and Damien. "Okay, fine. I do know the combination, and you tricked me into admitting it. But the axe was in the safe, so did you really expect me to tell you the truth about knowing how to get to it? I knew it would just make me look guilty."

"Because you are guilty," I said quietly. "You killed Mrs. Knowles because you thought she was endangering people. After she sold the knife to Orin, you went home that night and decided to murder her before she could cause harm to someone else." *And,* I added silently, *Fiona got the flash the moment you made up your mind.*

"She was going to get someone killed!" Wanda's voice began to rise until she was shouting. "Those items are magical! Dangerous! You might not believe in their power —she didn't believe, either—but that doesn't change what they are or what they can do! After I found out she had sold the knife, I couldn't take it anymore. I had to stop her!"

Bryce jerked backward, more popcorn flying as he stared at Wanda in shock. "You?" he breathed.

Wanda ignored him. Instead, she glared at me. When she spoke again, her voice was quieter and more controlled, almost a monotone. "Maledico tibi. Mors tibi. Mors maledictio!"

I nearly laughed, because it sounded like Wanda was trying to curse me, but it was unlike anything I had ever heard Morgan, Madge, and Maida say. It was almost silly. Cartoonish.

Something flashed in Wanda's hand, and I suddenly felt fear coursing through me, my urge to laugh utterly gone. Wanda lifted her hand, and I saw that her fingers were gripped tightly around a silver stake.

CHAPTER TWENTY-SEVEN

Damien stepped in front of me, one arm pushing me backward and the other coming up to grab Wanda's wrist. Before he could stop her, though, I saw her entire body go stiff. She froze, her hand still raised to slash with the stake. The only part of her that was moving was her eyes, which were wide with fear and confusion.

"Silly girl." The old woman's voice coming from my right was Morgan's, and I looked over to see her and the other two witches standing in a line. Each of them had one hand raised toward Wanda, their fingers splayed.

"Silly spell," Madge said.

"That's not magic," Maida said in her high voice. "This is."

Wanda's eyes slid left as she tried to look at the witches. With her unable to do any harm, I could turn my attention to Bryce. We had worried Orin's teeth might tip him off to the existence of supernatural creatures, but this, surely, had to be even more of a giveaway that there was more in the world than he knew about.

Except Bryce wasn't looking at the witches. He was staring at Wanda, looking appalled. Since she was facing Damien and me, Bryce circled around her and stepped in front of us. "Those items aren't dangerous," he said to Wanda. He sounded more sad than angry. "They never were. My father had those weapons for years, and they were harmless. You believe in all this occult and witchcraft stuff, but none of it is real."

Maida giggled.

Morgan's outstretched hand rotated, and her fingers flexed. Wanda began to cough, and for a moment, I worried Morgan was strangling her, but then Wanda spoke. Morgan had lifted the spell just enough that Wanda could move her mouth again.

"What are they doing to me?" Wanda's voice shook with fear.

"Nothing," Morgan said.

"At all," added Madge.

"You're free." Maida smiled sweetly.

With a jerk, Wanda's arm fell, the stake clattering to the ground. Damien reached past Bryce and grabbed it, then quickly slid it into the inside pocket of his suit coat.

Wanda looked down at her body and gave her limbs a little shake. "It *is* all real," she said icily. She pointed at the witches, but she was staring at Bryce. "Don't you see? Don't you understand why Cynthia had to be stopped?"

Bryce was shaking his head. "All I see is a murderer."

I didn't know if Bryce was in shock, too focused on Wanda to notice the magic that had happened right in front of him, or simply choosing to ignore what he couldn't understand. Whatever the reason was, at least we wouldn't have to take him aside for a little chat about the supernatural world.

And, as Bryce had said, we had a murderer right in front of us. We needed to call the police.

Even as I was thinking that, I looked over to see Damien with his phone to his ear. "Yes, by the concession stand," he was saying. "Where? Oh, I see. Yes, this way." He raised an arm and waved.

Officer Reyes was a short distance away, sprinting toward us with his cell phone in his hand.

"That was convenient," I said.

"I thought calling him might get us a faster response than dialing nine one one," Damien said, "but I didn't realize it would be this fast. How lucky he was already here."

"Very lucky."

Damien gave me a sidelong glance and asked quietly, "Unless you conjured it?"

I leaned toward Damien, keeping my voice low, too. "No, I've been too distracted by everything Wanda was telling us to even think about conjuring. Reyes being here is just a coincidence."

Speaking of Wanda, I realized she was no longer a threat. She certainly wasn't going to try to hurt me again, since she seemed to know the witches would never let her get away with it. I was sure she knew that trying to run would be a pointless effort, too.

Reyes kicked up a cloud of dust as he came to an abrupt halt in front of us. He looked between Wanda and Bryce, seemingly unsure whom he should be arresting.

"Officer Reyes," Damien said, "this woman has something to say."

"No, I don't," Wanda said. She crossed her arms.

"Oh, but she does," Morgan said.

"Something very important." Madge beamed at Reyes, who had turned to stare at the witches.

"She tried to kill Olivia just now." Maida pointed toward Damien. "He took the stake from her, though."

"Is that true?" Reyes asked Wanda, returning his attention to her.

"I'm allowed to have a lawyer," Wanda grumbled.

"We all heard you confess to killing Mrs. Knowles," Bryce said. His voice was calm. "We all saw you try to stab

Olivia, too." As surprising as his demeanor was, I was even more surprised to realize Bryce was still balancing his soda, hot dog, and popcorn. The box of popcorn was nearly half empty, but I had to commend the guy for hanging onto his food through everything that had just happened.

I might need a hot dog and a box of popcorn after all this drama.

"I was trying to shut her up," Wanda said quietly. She pointed her chin toward me. "She made me confess. She used her magic against me."

"I didn't," I told her honestly. As I had said to Damien, I had been far too distracted to focus on conjuring. "I just kept asking questions until I realized you had the combination to the safe. You were the only person other than Mrs. Knowles herself who could get to the axe stored inside it."

"You tricked me into admitting that."

I crossed my arms. "So you've said."

"You stole the axe and used it to kill Cynthia Knowles?" Reyes asked.

Wanda sighed. She nodded her head, almost imperceptibly. "I didn't think anyone would find it where I threw it."

"Luckily for us, you're not a good enough criminal to know how to properly dispose of a murder weapon." Reyes looked grim but satisfied. "Now, tell me, do you want to confess right here, or should we do it more formally at the station?"

Wanda's shoulders drooped. "It doesn't matter."

"The station it is, then." As Reyes put Wanda in handcuffs, I looked around and was surprised to realize a crowd had gathered around us. Some people even had their phones held up, taking photos or video of the arrest. I hoped very much that we hadn't been drawing any attention like that when the witches had used their magic to freeze Wanda.

I moved closer to Morgan. "Those words she said to

me. The ones that sounded like Latin. Did Wanda curse me?"

Morgan cackled. "Of course she didn't! That girl knows nothing of true witchcraft. You're perfectly safe. And, if someone ever does hex you, we can find a counter-spell for it. Don't you worry."

"I'm really glad you three were here today."

"I like baseball," Maida said.

"I know. That's fortunate for us," I told her. "We're going to get everyone at the Sanctuary together so we can play baseball with you."

"I'm going to hit a home run," Maida said confidently.

Damien stepped up to my side. "What I want to know is how you three arrived at just the right moment. Was that coincidence, or did you know we needed help?"

Madge tossed her blond curls over her shoulder. "We felt called. There was a need for protection."

"How does that even work?" I asked.

Madge smiled. "Your necklace. Who do you think put the protection spells on it?"

Maida looked like she was only about ten years old, but from things the witches had said before, I knew she was likely much older. Even Madge was a lot older than she looked. Baxter had given the necklace to Lucille at least forty years before. I knew it had to be that long ago because Damien had still been a baby when Lucille had ceased to exist in human form.

"You three." I said it like more of a question, since my brain had a hard time accepting the differences between the witches' appearances and their actual ages.

"Not just us," Morgan said. "There were others, too. Magic of all kinds has been bound to your necklace."

"And we felt it," Maida said. "Like a distress call, leading us to the necklace, and to you."

I pressed my fingers against the necklace. "Wow."

Damien had given it to me for protection, but I hadn't realized it was so powerful. That magic had possibly saved my life.

"Of course, Damien would have stopped her if we hadn't," Madge said.

Maida sighed. "By the way, I had the first week of June. If you could have waited until summer, I would have had fifty dollars to buy a pair of sneakers."

I smiled at Maida. "Damien and I will buy you a pair. As a thank-you for your help today."

Maida's face lit up. "Thank you! I'm going to go watch the rest of the game over there. But if someone else tries to kill you today, I'll come back and help again."

Maida turned and skipped toward the metal bleachers at one side of the nearest baseball diamond. Madge and Morgan followed more slowly, but they echoed Maida's promise.

Reyes had led Wanda away while Damien and I had been talking to the witches. Bryce was still standing a short distance away, staring into space.

"You okay?" I asked him.

"Not really," he admitted. "Who knew my father's collection would wind up being the reason someone got murdered?"

"Wanda's misguided sense of right and wrong is the reason someone was murdered," I corrected Bryce. Still, I could understand what he meant. If those hunter's weapons had never been sold to Mining Town Antiques, then Mrs. Knowles would still be alive.

"Why did your dad collect those things, anyway?" Damien asked.

"He picked up a few strange occult pieces on his travels, back when he was in the Army," Bryce said. "That was before he and my mom met. When I was little, we drove to Oregon one summer to visit some family. We went to a flea market, and that entire collection of weapons was for sale at one of the booths. My dad bought it, because he said the symbols meant they were used for occult rituals. He was fascinated by them, even though he never figured out what they were supposed to be used for. Like I told Wanda, they were harmless."

"Wanda didn't need any magic to kill with that axe," I pointed out. "They were dangerous weapons, whatever their original intended purpose might have been." And a hunter's weapon, I reminded myself, was just as deadly for a human as it was for a supernatural creature.

"Reyes said I have to go give a statement about what happened here today," Bryce said. "And he told me you two need to do the same."

I sighed. Of course we did. By that point, I was practically an expert at it.

Damien drove us to the police station, and when we went inside, Wanda and Reyes were still at the counter. It looked like Wanda's fingerprints had just been taken. She turned and spotted me, then said something to Reyes, who nodded his head.

Wanda's hands were cuffed in front of her, probably to make it easier to take her fingerprints, and she reached into the pocket of her jeans. "You asked me about the guy who bought the other knife," Wanda said to me. "He came back to the store yesterday, and he showed it to me, so I warned him he didn't know what he was dealing with. He said he knew exactly what he had in his hand, and to prove it, he gave me something. He said it was for luck, but it's obviously cursed."

Wanda pulled her hand out of her pocket, something gripped tightly in her fist. "You take it." Her breath hitched, and she suddenly looked like she was on the verge of tears. "Please. I'm afraid to keep it."

She really thinks Orin gave her a cursed object. Even if Wanda was correct, the witches had just promised they could undo anything, so I stepped forward and held out my hand, palm up. Wanda dropped a white embroidered handkerchief into my hand.

I unfolded the handkerchief. Inside was a bright red feather that shimmered in the light. The tips faded to a brilliant orange.

As I lifted the feather to look at it more closely, Wanda said, "He claimed it was a phoenix feather, but everyone knows phoenixes aren't real."

CHAPTER TWENTY-EIGHT

"Come on, Ms. Jordan," Reyes said. He guided Wanda through the doors that I knew led to the Nightmare Police Department's jail cells.

I barely paid any attention. I was too busy staring at the feather. "Damien," I said under my breath, "do you think it's really what she says?"

Damien gently took the feather and held it up. He turned it first one way, then the other, and the shimmer made it look like the feather was dancing in the air. "Let's give our statements," he said.

In other words, the middle of the police station wasn't the place to discuss whether or not this feather had really come from a phoenix. And, if it had, whether that phoenix was Damien's father.

I nodded, then held out the handkerchief so we could rewrap the feather. I tucked it inside my purse, then began to wait very impatiently for Reyes or another officer to call for us. Bryce joined us a few minutes later—he was obviously a much slower driver than Damien—and the three of us sat in silence in the station's small waiting area, too absorbed in our own thoughts to talk.

It wasn't until Damien laid a hand on my leg that I realized I had been tapping my foot against the floor. I stopped and whispered, "Sorry."

"I'm about two minutes away from running laps around the building," he answered. "I want to get this over with, too, so we can get to the important stuff."

"Solving a murder is pretty important, too," I said, even though I knew exactly what he meant. He was anxious to find out if that feather would lead us to answers about Baxter.

Damien's hand slid into mine. "Yes, it is. I'm really proud of you, Olivia. You figured it out." He leaned toward me and gave me a quick kiss.

As it turned out, Damien didn't have to resort to running laps. Reyes came out and called him into his office less than a minute later. After that, it was my turn.

When I sat down opposite Reyes, he looked at me seriously. "Your talents are wasted at that haunted house," he said.

I thought he was kidding at first, but there was no trace of humor in his expression or tone. "I'm not going to the police academy any time soon, Luis," I answered. "I'm happy at the Sanctuary. Besides, I have talents outside of finding dead bodies, you know."

Reyes smiled. "I know. Speaking of Nightmare Sanctuary, is your friend Justine seeing anyone?"

I stifled a laugh. "You can ask her that yourself. Now, can we please get this statement over with?"

Not too long after, Damien and I were on our way to the Sanctuary. The second we had gotten in his car, we started discussing the feather.

"We have no reason to think Orin was lying about what it is," Damien said. "The question is, where did he get it?"

"And why would he give it to Wanda? Surely he would have known we'd find out about it."

Damien shook his head as he pulled out of the police station parking lot. "Why would we find out? We're not friends with Wanda. And I doubt Orin realizes just how good you are at digging up clues. I'm sure he never suspected you'd wind up with the feather."

"What's our plan?" I asked.

"We're going to have a serious chat with Orin." Damien paused. "After we get some backup."

Damien raced to the Sanctuary, and he took one turn so quickly I had to brace myself against the door. If there had been any police cars on the road, we would have wound up back at the station in no time, sitting in jail cells of our own for speeding. Damien parked right in front of the building's entrance and practically ran inside.

The first place Damien went was Zach's office, but the door was locked. I had lingered in the entryway, so when Damien returned, I started up the stairs with him on my heels. We found Gunnar and Zach sitting in front of Fiona and Seraphina's door, clearly on guard duty.

"We need you two and Malcolm," Damien said without preamble.

"Malcolm is out back, keeping an eye on Orin," Zach said. "He's been wandering the grounds."

"Doesn't someone need to watch over Sera?" Gunnar asked.

"We're going to have a long talk with Orin. She'll be safe." Damien was already turning to head back down the stairs. As he went, he pulled his phone out of his pocket. I assumed he was calling Malcolm to find out exactly where we should go.

Zach and Gunnar passed me, and I felt the wind kicked up by Gunnar's wings as he flexed them in anticipation of the confrontation. He was ready for a fight, not a conversation. I followed as quickly as I could, but even still, the others were already going out the back door by the time I reached the ground floor.

When I got outside, I saw Malcolm striding toward

Damien, Gunnar, and Zach. He pointed a long finger in the direction of a trail that led to the cemetery that had once been for hospital patients who died at the Sanctuary.

Everyone slowed, their heads close together as they talked quietly. It gave me a chance to catch up, and I heard Damien say firmly, "We're just talking to him. Not accusing him."

"Or fighting him?" Zach asked, sounding a little disappointed.

"Definitely not," Damien said.

We followed the trail and found Orin striding through the cemetery, walking along a row of graves. He looked bored.

Damien reached the low iron gate that surrounded the cemetery before he called Orin's name. Orin looked up, and as soon as he realized there was a whole group of us, he frowned and looked around, like he was trying to find an exit.

I pulled the handkerchief from my purse as we walked up to Orin, who had stopped walking and was standing facing us, his hands curled into loose fists. I threaded my way between Malcolm's shoulder and Gunnar's left wing, then held up the feather. "Where did you get this?" I asked.

Orin's body stiffened as he stared at the feather. "Where did you get it?" he countered.

"Wanda, the woman at the antique store, passed it along. You gave it to her."

Orin crossed his arms over his chest. "I bought it. From a guy."

"You're going to have to tell us more than that," Damien said.

"I don't have to tell you anything." Orin was moving before he had even finished speaking. He sprinted down the row of graves, cut left, and jumped the fence. He skirted the perimeter of the cemetery until he reached the trail that led back to the Sanctuary. Gunnar, Zach, Malcolm, and Damien were already running after him.

"Really? More running?" I said to myself as I followed at a slower pace.

I emerged from the trail to see Orin sprinting across the back lawn of the Sanctuary. Instead of going inside, he was going to run around the building. Malcolm was nearly on him, but before he could tackle Orin, the sound of a woman singing reached my ears. The voice was beautiful, though the high notes were almost painfully loud. Ahead of me, I saw everyone but Orin clap their hands over their ears.

Seraphina and Fiona were at the back door. Seraphina was bracing herself against the edge of her rolling tank, her head lifted toward the sky. The singing was coming from her. I wasn't sure if sirens could mesmerize women the way they could men, but just in case, I covered my ears, too.

Orin slowed as he began to raise his hands to his ears, but he was too late. The siren's song was already taking hold of him, and he stopped and turned toward Seraphina. His face went slack, and his arms lowered to his sides.

Gunnar hurried toward Orin, and Seraphina stopped singing just as Gunnar uncovered his ears so he could grab Orin from behind. Even with the spell broken, Orin didn't put up much of a fight. Still, Gunnar continued to hold onto him as the rest of us moved in front of them.

"Tell me more about the guy you bought the feather from," Damien prompted.

"He told me there are plenty of these for the taking, if you know where to look." Orin was angry, but at least he was talking. "When Gunnar reached out to me, I knew the feathers must be coming from Baxter. I came to Nightmare hoping to pick up his trail."

"You didn't want to help us find him," Damien said. "You wanted to find him for yourself. And you arrived in Nightmare a day early to scout things out."

Orin shrugged as best he could when he had two massive arms pinning him in place. "The guy I got the feather from is with the Night Runners, the faction looking to make a power move. Having a phoenix on hand could help with that, which meant my contact was getting the feathers from his own people, though he said he didn't know who among them actually has the creature. I wanted to find out so I could either make an alliance or take it from them."

"Not *it*," Zach growled. "Him. Baxter."

"They have my father in captivity, and they've forced him to return to his bird form." Damien looked like he was using every inch of willpower not to lash out at Orin. "Give me the name of the man who sold you the feather."

Orin hesitated, and Malcolm slid closer to him. "I suggest you do as he says."

"Or what?" Orin spat out a laugh. "All of you are too tame to kill me."

"You don't know what I am, do you?" Malcolm leaned forward at the waist until his face was just inches from Orin's.

Orin was right: no one at the Sanctuary was going to hurt or kill him. Still, there must have been something in Malcolm's face that made him doubt that, because his eyes flicked from Malcolm to Damien. "Lars. His name is Lars Bancroft."

Malcolm stepped back. "Thank you."

Fiona had been slowly pushing Seraphina's tank toward us, water sloshing out as it rattled over the uneven ground. Seraphina leaned over the top of her tank to glare at Orin. "What do we do with him now?"

CHAPTER TWENTY-NINE

"Orin, you will leave Nightmare just as soon as you have told us how to contact Lars." Damien's eyes flashed. "You will never come to this town again, and you will not attempt to take or hold my father captive. Do you understand?"

"You're letting him go?" Fiona asked incredulously.

"We'll escort him to the city limits." Damien looked at Fiona. "We're not monsters, unlike the people who took my father."

Seraphina sighed. "Sometimes doing the right thing is no fun."

Malcolm and Zach volunteered to be Orin's escort, since Gunnar would be too conspicuous. A gargoyle couldn't just cruise through town in the middle of the day. Malcolm and Zach quickly hustled Orin inside so he could pack his things and hand over contact information for Lars Bancroft.

Once the three of them were gone, Seraphina relaxed. "I sure hope he stays gone."

"I think he will," Damien said confidently.

"This lead is helpful," Fiona said. "I used to know someone who would occasionally buy things from the Night Runners, and I can ask about her contacts. Between

Gunnar and me, and this guy Lars, we'll be able to find out who has Baxter."

"This is the closest we've been to finding him," Gunnar said. "I'm just sorry we had to go through so much to get to this point. Sera, I will be apologizing to you for the next century."

Seraphina waved a hand, spraying water drops across Gunnar's chest. "It was worth it. No apology necessary."

"Mrs. Knowles died because of Orin," Damien said sadly.

"Mrs. Knowles died because Wanda was terribly misguided," I said. "Orin just happened to be the customer who sent her over the edge. If it hadn't been him, it would have been someone else. It's a shame Wanda's beliefs led her to murder."

"She wasn't wrong that magical items in the hands of the wrong person can be dangerous," Damien said. "Except the very items she was so worried about weren't even magical."

"Hold on a second," Gunnar said. "You found the killer?"

"Olivia did," Damien said proudly.

Gunnar gave me an appreciative nod. "We have a lot of catching up to do."

"We sure do," I agreed. "It's been quite a day. We found the killer, the witches saved my life, and I was given a phoenix feather that might be from Baxter."

"I thought the witches were at a baseball game?" Seraphina asked.

"Let's go inside," Damien suggested. He slid his arm around my waist and gave me a teasing look. "The way Olivia was eyeing a box of popcorn earlier, I'm guessing she'd like to tell our story over a late lunch."

We began to move in the direction of the back door as Gunnar sighed deeply. I thought he was feeling guilty about all the drama Orin's visit had caused until he said, "I was really hoping to win that fifty bucks."

"You and I are the hot gossip," I told Damien.

"I don't mind." Damien smiled at me. "Now that we know my power manifests when I'm very happy, I expect I'll learn a lot more about my abilities. That's good, because if we're going to infiltrate a black-market faction and free my father, then we have a lot of practicing to do. But first, let's eat!"

A NOTE FROM THE AUTHOR

When I'm working on a manuscript, I give each chapter a short name that describes what happens in it. That way, when I'm editing, it's easier to find the scene I'm looking for. So, for example, chapter nine is named "Mama Gossips." Chapter twenty-two's name is a word that I'm sure many of you said or thought while you were reading *that* scene: "FINALLY!" Believe me, I feel the same way, and I hope you're as happy with how events played out as I am.

And, as always, will you please leave a review for *Axing at the Antique Store*? It really means so much to me!

Eternally Yours,

Beth

P.S. You can keep up with my latest book news, get fun freebies, and more by signing up for my newsletter at Beth-Dolgner.com!

Fatality at the *Festival*

NIGHTMARE, ARIZONA BOOK EIGHT
PARANORMAL COZY MYSTERIES

Crystals, corn dogs, and crime in Nightmare, Arizona.

Olivia Kendrick is excited about Nightmare's annual arts and crafts festival until a vendor winds up dead inside his food truck. Locals and festival artists alike disliked the corn dog seller, but who had enough motive to murder him?

The supernatural community at Nightmare Sanctuary Haunted House must pull together to help gather clues, from a siren on a spy mission to witches with connections. Even Felipe the chupacabra is sniffing for clues!

As Olivia gets closer to the truth about the murder, she also gets a cryptic clue about the whereabouts of Damien Shackleford's missing father, Baxter. Nightmare's favorite amateur sleuth and her paranormal friends must put the pieces together before it's too late…

ACKNOWLEDGMENTS

I'm going to work backward this time, starting with the last people who see a book before it goes out into the world. To my team of ARC readers: thank you for your continued support and reviews. You helped my last book hit number one in one of its categories! Jena at BookMojo makes everything look pretty, including the cover design. Lia at Your Best Book Editor and Trish at Blossoming Pages handle my editing with skill and patience. And, of course, my test readers find plot holes, call out weird phrasing, and generally keep me in line, so I'm sending lots of love to Alex, Sabrina, Lisa, Kristine, Mom, and David.

ABOUT THE AUTHOR

Beth Dolgner writes paranormal fiction and nonfiction. Her interest in things that go bump in the night really took off on a trip to Savannah, Georgia, so it's fitting that her first series—Betty Boo, Ghost Hunter—takes place in that spooky city. Beth also writes paranormal nonfiction, including her first book, *Georgia Spirits and Specters*, which is a collection of Georgia ghost stories.

Beth and her husband, Ed, live in Tucson, Arizona. They're close enough to Tombstone that Beth can easily visit its Wild West street and watch staged shootouts, all in the name of research for the Nightmare, Arizona series.

Beth also enjoys giving presentations on Victorian death and mourning traditions as well as Victorian Spiritualism. She has been a volunteer at an historic cemetery, a ghost tour guide, and a paranormal investigator.

Keep up with Beth and sign up for her newsletter at BethDolgner.com.

BOOKS BY BETH DOLGNER

The Nightmare, Arizona Series

Paranormal Cozy Mystery

Homicide at the Haunted House

Drowning at the Diner

Slaying at the Saloon

Murder at the Motel

Poisoning at the Party

Headless at Halloween (Novella)

Clawing at the Corral

Axing at the Antique Store

Fatality at the Festival

The Eternal Rest Bed and Breakfast Series

Paranormal Cozy Mystery

Sweet Dreams

Late Checkout

Picture Perfect

Scenic Views

Breakfast Included

Groups Welcome

Quiet Nights

Halloween Vibes (Novella)

The Betty Boo, Ghost Hunter Series

Romantic Urban Fantasy

Ghost of a Threat

Ghost of a Whisper

Ghost of a Memory

Ghost of a Hope

Manifest

Young Adult Steampunk

A Talent for Death

Young Adult Urban Fantasy

Nonfiction

Georgia Spirits and Specters

Everyday Voodoo